"Can we call a tru[...] [...]u
with your ankle."

Chloe blew her long bangs away from her eyes. The sincerity in Trevor Montgomery's deep green eyes stirred something inside her. She wanted to trust him, to believe in him. She hadn't felt that way in a long time. What choice did she have anyway? Taking his hand, she shook it firmly. "Truce. . .for now."

"Good." He pushed the automatic button to roll down his window. "I didn't know how much longer I could hold my breath." Looking at her, he waved his hand in front of his nose. "You stink."

Her mouth dropped open. Without thinking, she punched his arm. "I can't believe you just said that."

"Truth hurts sometimes." He started the car then looked at her. "If it makes you feel any better, you *look* cute—a little disheveled but cute just the same."

She leaned back in the chair. Somehow that did make her feel better, but she'd never, not in a million years, admit it to him.

JENNIFER JOHNSON and her unbelievably supportive husband, Albert, are happily married and raising Brooke, Hayley, and Allie, the three cutest young ladies on the planet. Besides being a middle school teacher, Jennifer loves to read, write, and chauffeur her girls. She is a member of American Christian Fiction Writers. Blessed beyond measure, Jennifer hopes to always think like a child—bigger than imaginable and with complete faith. Send her a note at jenwrites4god@bellsouth.net.

Books by Jennifer Johnson

HEARTSONG PRESENTS
HP725—By His Hand
HP738—Picket Fence Pursuit

Pursuing
the Goal

Jennifer Johnson

Heartsong Presents

To my middle daughter, Hayley. How many soccer and basketball games have we attended? Too many to count! I've relished every minute. I'm so thankful for your sweet, sensitive spirit. May you always strive for the best goal—Jesus.

Thank you to my husband, Albert, who has supported and encouraged me every moment on this journey, as well as my girls, Brooke, Hayley, and Allie, who spent fall break being very patient and allowing Mom to write half of each day to meet the deadline. Rose McCauley, you are a gem. Your quick crits have been a lifesaver! Most important, thank You, my Lord and Savior, for saving me, loving me, and guiding my life, for wrapping Your arms around me when I've needed You most. May my life reflect You.

A note from the Author:
I love to hear from my readers! You may correspond with me by writing:

Jennifer Johnson
Author Relations
PO Box 721
Uhrichsville, OH 44683

ISBN 978-1-59789-625-2

PURSUING THE GOAL

Our mission is to publish and distribute inspirational products offering exceptional value and biblical encouragement to the masses.

one

Chloe Andrews watched the soccer ball fly toward her then used her hip to push an opposing teammate out of the way. With the ball about to land a few feet in front of her, she moved forward then turned and arched her back, forcing the ball to roll down her chest. She took control of the sphere with her foot then pivoted and dribbled around the fullback—the last player before the goal. Taking a split-second glance toward the coaches on the sidelines, Chloe smiled in satisfaction. *They're watching.*

She turned her attention to the goalie, one of her close friends on Ball State University's soccer team who was also playing for the opposition in this practice scrimmage. Squinting her eyes, Chloe studied the target. Renee could dive with precision to the right of the goal. Her weakness was the left. Zeroing in on the left corner, Chloe dribbled another step, twisted her hip then smashed the ball with her right foot. It zoomed toward its destination, and Renee jumped, arms extended over her head. But Chloe's kick was hard, and the ball smashed into the net. Score!

"Yes!" Chloe pumped her fist through the air. A teammate scrimmaging on her side ran up to her for a high five.

"Ten-minute break. Get some water!" Coach Collins yelled from the sidelines.

Chloe headed toward the table that held the sports drink container and plastic cups. She felt a shove from behind. Chloe turned, and Renee grinned. "I knew you had me."

"What can I say? When you got it, you got it." Teasing, she blew on her fingertips then brushed them against her shoulder.

Renee laughed. "I suppose." With the back of her gloved hand, she wiped sweat from her forehead. "It's barely ten o' clock, and I'm about to suffocate out here."

"It is super hot, even for August in Indiana." Chloe fanned the front of her soppy T-shirt. She grabbed a glass of water, took a good swig, and dumped the rest over her head. "We still have an hour left."

Renee groaned. "Don't remind me." She took a drink. "How was your visit with your family?"

"Good enough, I guess. One of my brothers, Dalton, had to make a trip to Indianapolis for something. I met him and his wife and kids up there for dinner." She shrugged. "Don't get me wrong. I love to visit with my nephews and nieces and everyone, but I just don't feel I really belong."

"Why?"

"I don't know." She threw her cup into the plastic trash bag. "Probably 'cause all they ever talk about is God-this and God-that. I get tired of it."

"Humph. I would, too. Why don't you just tell them you don't want to hear about it?"

"They'd die." Chloe looked away from Renee. All the Andrews family ever wanted to do was talk about the wonderful blessings God had given them, be it another baby, a good job, safety in the coal mines, at school, going to the grocery. They praised God for every little thing they did. If they walked out the front door and didn't get hit by a truck, they were praising God about it. They really got on Chloe's nerves.

The funny thing was, the Andrews clan, as people liked to

call them, all believed Chloe agreed with their sentiments on God. In truth Chloe thought God was great. She loved to hear stories about Him when she was growing up, but her true comfort had always come from her soccer ball. After a long day at school or a breakup with a boyfriend or a day when Daddy was coughing extra hard battling black lung disease, Chloe would go outside and dribble her soccer ball. It was always there for her—sure and steady.

Renee nudged Chloe's arm. "Did you see the new assistant athletic trainer?"

Chloe shook her head.

"That man is hotter than the sun beating down on our backs." Renee smiled. "Take a look at him. He's standing by Coach Collins."

Chloe glanced at the man towering several inches above her coach's short stature. Sporting a red Ball State T-shirt and black shorts, the new guy looked to be in pretty good shape, but Chloe couldn't distinguish anything about his facial features or even his hair color with the Cardinals cap planted on his head. "How can you tell?"

Renee wiggled her eyebrows. "I've seen him up close." She nudged Chloe's arm with her elbow. "And he is sizzling."

Chloe threw back her head and laughed. "Are you sure he's a mere mortal?"

"Girl, I'm telling you—I'm not sure."

"You stay here and drool." Chloe slid her left foot around a nearby soccer ball and shimmied it with ease in front of her. "I'm heading onto the field to impress Coach Jiminy Cricket—I mean Jimmy Collins."

"You'd better not let Coach hear you say that. You'll be running around this field until you're puking your guts out."

Chloe winked and motioned for Renee to follow her onto

the field. "Come on. I'm gonna score another on ya."

Renee threw her cup in the trash. "Wouldn't doubt it."

❧

Trevor Montgomery lifted the baseball cap off his head then wiped the perspiration from his brow. Though soccer had been his passion for as long as he could remember, he couldn't deny he liked the sport much better once the weather turned a bit cooler. Placing the cap back on his head, he scanned the field for Sarah, the fullback he'd been guiding through physical therapy the last few months. Her knee had healed nicely since her surgery in May, but Trevor felt confident the girl wouldn't be back to full ability for another several weeks.

A tall girl zoomed past him. Though obviously muscular, her build was much thinner than her teammates'. She reminded him more of a model than a soccer player—until he watched the ball shuffling between her feet as if it had always belonged there. "Her control is amazing."

Coach Collins nodded, and a slight grin bowed his lips. "Yep. She's pretty awesome, all right. We've put twenty pounds on her in the four years we've had her."

"What?"

The coach smacked his gum and nodded. "You heard me right. Chloe was thin as a blade of grass when we picked her up from a small school in Otwell, Indiana, but, boy, could that gal dribble and shoot."

Trevor watched as Chloe kicked the soccer ball, nailing it into the goal. Her long, sandy-brown hair whipped around her face as she turned and high-fived one of her teammates.

"Got me again." The goalie scooped the ball from inside the net and threw it to the middle. "But I've figured you out, friend. That's the last one."

Trevor smiled when the tall beauty shrugged her shoulders and blew her friend a kiss. She moved like a gazelle with graceful motions back to the center of the field. "She's a senior, huh?"

"Yep. I'll hate to see her go. Works hard. Couldn't ask for a more coachable player." He smacked his gum again. "Does everything I ask. No questions. No complaints."

༄

"What Coach don't know won't hurt him." Chloe bent down and untucked her shoelaces from inside the tops of her cleats.

"Chloe, you can't take those laces out. It's Coach's biggest pet peeve." Liz, Chloe's other roommate and one of the fullbacks for the team, pushed her hair behind her ear. "Where are your Sweet Spots anyway?"

Chloe visualized her candy-red, thick rubber bands sitting on top of her dresser. Sweet Spots were the best invention to the soccer world in Chloe's opinion. A player simply had to shimmy the thick rubber over the cleat and the band would hold the shoelaces in place on top of the shoe. No shoestrings poking into a player's foot beneath the lip of the cleats. "I was in a hurry and forgot them."

"If you break your leg. . ."

Chloe stood to her full height of five feet eleven inches, towering over her teammate. "I'm not going to break my leg."

"Okay." Liz lifted her hands in surrender. "Don't say I didn't warn you."

Walking back to center field, Chloe peeked at Coach Collins. He seemed deep in conversation with the trainer. She had to admit the new guy's height alone attracted her a bit. Most men were barely as tall as she. Not that she cared too much for the opposite sex anyway. Her hometown football king, Randy Reynolds, had made sure of that. She hoped he was happy with his snooty, prom-queen wife whose daddy owned a coal mine back home in Otwell. The last thing Chloe heard was that Randy had a strapping young son and another baby on the way.

A growl formed deep in her throat. Money had obviously meant more than every ounce of affection and love she had conjured for the overgrown country boy. *I'm glad he broke it off with me. I probably would have done something stupid like marry him right out of high school.* She took her position as center forward. *And I'd have missed out on this.*

The whistle blew to start the scrimmage again. Molly, the new sophomore center forward, dribbled the ball past Chloe. *I gotta keep an eye on that one.* Chloe turned and watched as Molly maneuvered the ball toward the goal. Having transferred from a small community college in Kentucky, Molly made a great second-string center forward. Chloe had every intention of making sure the gal stayed second string, at least until Chloe graduated.

Liz stole the ball from Molly and kicked it hard toward Chloe. Chloe ran forward to meet it. She tripped. Sharp, hot pain seared through her ankle. She fell forward toward the grass carpet. A piercing scream rang through her ears. In disbelief she realized it was her own.

two

Trevor watched the color drain from Coach Collins's face. "Oh no! That girl never gets hurt!" He dropped his clipboard to the ground and sprinted onto the field.

Trevor turned and saw the tall girl the coach had called Chloe sitting on the ground with both hands wrapped around her foot. She rocked back and forth, scrunching her face in agony. Trevor ran toward her. He bent down next to Coach Collins. "What hurts?"

"My foot. My ankle." She spit the words through clenched teeth. A tear slipped from her squinted eyes.

"Your shoe's untied." Coach Collins growled. "Where're your Sweet Spots?"

"Sorry, Coach." She swiped her eyes with the back of her hand. "I'm okay. Just a little twist."

"Now wait a minute." Coach placed his hand on her shoulder. "Let's let Trevor take a look at it."

"I think I know my own body." Her eyes flashed with an anger Trevor knew was a mask for her pain. Despite Coach's warning, she tried to put pressure on her foot then let out a screeching howl.

"Here, Chloe." Trevor kept his voice calm but firm. Her gaze locked with his as he gently grabbed her cleat and began to loosen the untied shoestrings. She was obviously not one to willingly heed instruction, but heed it she must. Trevor never took his gaze from hers. A challenge flicked beneath her stubborn baby blues. Amused, he almost allowed a snicker to escape his lips. Almost. She'd started the staring war, and he'd be the one to finish it.

Without looking away, he pulled her sock off her foot. He grabbed the shin guard and slowly shimmied it down her leg. He watched as she sucked in her breath and scrunched her eyes shut when the protective piece touched her ankle. Looking down, he noted that her ankle and the top of her foot had already begun to swell. *Definitely a sprain. She may have a break. I hope it's not broken, Lord. It's obvious soccer means a lot to her.*

"That doesn't look good," Coach whispered and wiped his hand across his sweat-covered face.

"I think it would be best if I take her to the hospital to get an X-ray." Trevor tried to keep his tone optimistic, yet he could already tell from the severity of the swelling that Chloe would be out a couple of weeks in the best of scenarios.

"No, I'm fine." A sob spilled from her lips.

A short, stocky girl leaned toward another player and murmured, "I've never seen Chloe like this."

"I didn't even know she could cry," the other responded.

Chloe must have heard, as well, because she pushed away from him and tried to stand once more. "I'm fine. I know I'm—" She fell forward on her knees when she tried to put her weight on her injured foot.

"Okay. I've had enough of this." Trevor stood and swooped the woman into his arms.

"What do you think you're doing?" Her tear-splattered eyes widened in surprise.

"I'm getting you out of here. Taking you to the hospital." He turned and looked at Coach Collins. "I've got her. I'll call your cell as soon as I know something."

Coach Collins nodded and clapped his hands together. "All

right. Show's over. Back to practice."

"I don't want you to carry me." A strong fist pounded into the back of his shoulder. "I'm okay." Her body shook in his arms as sobs overtook her. "I have to be."

He was surprised when she rested her face on his chest. She was obviously a strong woman, but he sensed her vulnerability. Everything in him wanted to protect her from her pain and embarrassment.

Once they were beside his car, he lowered her to her feet, making sure her weight was balanced on the uninjured foot. "Everything will be fine." He fished through the pocket of his shorts, pulled out his car keys, and unlocked the door. "I'll get you back on that field—"

"Your shirt!" She interrupted him, a look of horror on her face.

He glanced down at his red shirt and saw the enormous wet blotch across the front. He shrugged. "No big deal. Just tears."

"Yeah. Mine." She bit her bottom lip so hard Trevor feared she'd draw blood. "I don't cry."

"It'll dry in no time." He gently nudged her into the car and walked around to the driver's side. Slipping inside, he smiled at her. "I know. I've got another in the back." He jumped out of the car and grabbed a white polo from the backseat. Black running shorts and a polo shirt weren't exactly the best of matches, but he didn't want Chloe to be any more embarrassed than she already was.

≈

Chloe knew her face had to be ten shades of red. *How could I have tripped over my own two feet? Now some guy I don't even know had to change his shirt because I cried all over it.* Chloe Andrews was a leader. People looked up to her. She was strong, not a babbling crybaby. She gazed out the front window, willing him to hurry so they could leave the field. The knowledge that her teammates sneaked peeks toward his car made her feel furious and humiliated all at the same time.

He slid back into the driver's seat. "Sorry."

"For what?" She tapped her fingers against the door handle.

"I didn't mean to embarrass you again."

Unwilling to let him think he could get the best of Chloe Andrews, she faced him. "You didn't embarrass me."

"I just didn't want you to feel uncomfortable with your tears on my shirt."

My tears on his shirt. Oh, the very notion of it made her blood boil. "What do I care if my tears got on your shirt? You didn't need to go change or anything. It was just a tiny spot."

A deep, guttural laugh filled his car. "Someone doesn't handle being vulnerable very well."

"Excuse me?" Heat enveloped her once more. How dare he try to psychoanalyze her! She hadn't asked for his opinion, hadn't even asked for him to help her off the field. She reached for the door handle. "I will not be laughed at."

The overgrown trainer touched something on the side of his door, and a click sounded throughout the car. "You're not going anywhere but to the hospital."

"I am not a child, Mr.—whatever your last name is. I believe I know how to unlock a door." She tried to flip the lock, but it wouldn't budge.

"Not in this car."

She glared at him. A smile that reminded her very much of the Cheshire cat from *Alice in Wonderland* formed on his lips.

"It's childproof. Once I lock the door on my side, you can't get out on yours. By the way, my last name is Montgomery." He extended his hand toward her. "Can we call a truce? I'd really like to help you with your ankle."

Chloe blew her long bangs away from her eyes. The sincerity in Trevor Montgomery's deep green eyes stirred something inside her. She wanted to trust him, to believe in him. She hadn't felt that way in a long time. What choice did she have anyway? Taking his hand, she shook it firmly. "Truce. . .for now."

"Good." He pushed the automatic button to roll down his window. "I didn't know how much longer I could hold my breath." Looking at her, he waved his hand in front of his nose. "You stink."

Her mouth dropped open. Without thinking, she punched his arm. "I can't believe you just said that."

"Truth hurts sometimes." He started the car then looked at her. "If it makes you feel any better, you *look* cute—a little disheveled but cute just the same."

She leaned back in the chair. Somehow that did make her feel better, but she'd never, not in a million years, admit it to him.

❧

"There is no way I am staying off my foot for six weeks!"

Trevor watched in dismay as the young woman who represented Ball State's best hope for a winning season threw a wad of gauze at the young doctor who'd come into the room to tell Chloe the diagnosis for her foot.

"I can't wait six weeks. Our first game is in two." She picked up a roll of tape.

"Miss Andrews!" The doctor snatched the tape from her hand. "You are not a child. This is a sterile environment. One that demands your respect—"

Trevor reached for the doctor's arm as Chloe picked up a plastic bedpan. Confident she'd sail that through the air, as well, he pulled the doctor into the hall. "Tell me what you've found." He pulled out his Ball State ID. "I'll be her trainer. Let me tell her, and I'll deal with her."

The doctor exhaled and rubbed the back of his neck. "This is my first night for my emergency room residency." He glanced at his watch. "I guess I should say morning. It's almost lunchtime, and I haven't even had breakfast. No wonder my stomach's growling." He half chuckled, half sighed then looked at Trevor. "Between the child who threw up on me and the irate father who expressed his opinion in not the kindest of words, I am completely worn out."

"Don't worry. You'll develop a tough shell."

"So they tell me." He crossed his arms in front of his chest, letting the package Trevor assumed he'd prepared for Chloe dangle at his side. "I hope I don't get too hardened. My plan is to finish up and head over to Africa."

Trevor's curiosity was piqued. "For?"

"Missions work. I'd like to give medical care and witness to others at the same time." He uncrossed his arms. "Anyway. . ."

"I think that's wonderful. I'll pray for you."

"You're a Christian?"

Trevor rocked back on his heels. "Oh yes. My calling is to work from the sidelines, help ball players heal from injury, and share my faith every chance I get. My prayer is to get a job back home at the University of South Carolina, working for the Fighting Gamecocks."

"I'll pray for you, too." He let out a long breath. "This has been the highlight of my shift. Always good to get an encouraging reminder of why we need to keep going."

"Definitely. So what's the diagnosis?"

"Third-degree sprain."

"Ruptured ligaments?"

"Yes."

"She's going to need a cast?"

"Yes."

"A removable air cast will be good enough?"

"You know your stuff." The doctor chuckled and handed the package to Trevor. "I think an air cast will be enough. I'm going to prescribe some anti-inflammatory medicine for her." He pulled a pad out of his jacket pocket and scribbled a prescription on the top sheet. He handed it to Trevor. "I want her to stay completely off the ankle for two full weeks. After that you can begin her on some physical therapy."

Trevor scratched his chin and nodded. "Sounds good." He glanced at the door and took a deep breath.

"At least it wasn't broken."

"I agree." Trevor pointed to the door. "But I don't think she will."

The doctor patted Trevor's shoulder. "Have fun." He waved and walked down the hall. "I'll say a prayer for you with her, as well."

Trevor half smiled as he pushed open the door. His heart melted at the sight of Chloe sitting on the bed with her shoulders slumped and her gaze locked on the ground. Strands of once-sweaty hair had escaped her long, light brown ponytail and now stuck out around her head at odd angles. She was a complete mess, yet Trevor was drawn to her as he'd never been drawn to a woman before.

"Chloe?"

"Yeah."

She didn't look up at him, just sat still on the bed. He opened the package containing the air cast then knelt in front of her and fastened the cast to her foot.

"Come on." Trevor scooped her into his arms once more.

"What are you doing?" The fight had fled from her voice. Frustration and defeat replaced it.

"I'm taking you home." Trevor lowered her into the wheelchair just outside the door. To his surprise she didn't argue, allowing him to push her to his car. Once she was nestled under her seat belt, he slipped into the driver's seat and drove away. Only able to get her address from her, Trevor focused on getting her home. He'd take her into the apartment and talk to her there.

After pulling into the lot, he jumped out and scurried over to her side. She opened the door and pointed toward the third apartment door. "There's a key under the mat."

"Okay. I'll open the door then come back for you."

She nodded, and he made his way to the apartment. Her quiet defeat was worse than her irrational fire. *She's probably a ticking time bomb that's going to blow the minute I tell her the prognosis.* After unlocking the door, he walked back to the car, lifted her out of it, and carried her into the apartment. He set her on the couch.

She clasped her hands in her lap and stared up at him. The fire was back. Not only could he see it; he could feel it. "How bad is it?"

"Well. . ."

"Broken?"

"No."

Though she probably hadn't meant for him to see it, Trevor watched her shoulders fall in relief. "Sprained?"

"Yes."

A smile warmed her face. Trevor couldn't help but notice how her eyes smiled with her lips. The expression was one of the sweetest he'd ever seen. "That's not so bad. I'll walk it off."

Trevor shook his head. "No, Chloe. This is a third-degree

sprain. You've ruptured ligaments. You'll need to wear an air cast and rest it completely for two weeks. Then I'll begin you on some physical therapy. You should be ready to play in about six—"

"Our first game is in two weeks."

Trevor stared into her eyes. "You'll have to miss it."

"No. I won't."

Trevor spoke calmly but firmly. "Yes, Chloe. If you don't rest your ankle and stay off it for the next two weeks, you'll make the injury worse and prolong your recovery."

She shook her head. "I'll be back on that field in a week."

"No." The phone rang on the end table beside Chloe. It rang again. "Are you going to pick it up?"

"No."

"Why?"

"It's my mom, and I don't want to talk."

Trevor smiled. He'd tell her mother about the injury. Maybe she could talk some sense into Chloe. Before she realized what he was doing, Trevor swiped the receiver off the table. "Hello."

"Hello?" The woman on the other end sounded confused. "I believe I've called the wrong number."

"Are you trying to reach Chloe Andrews?"

Chloe grabbed his arm and whispered through clenched teeth. "What do you think you're doing?"

Trevor covered the phone with his hand. "Telling your mother."

"You will not." Chloe tried to grab it from his hand, but Trevor stepped out of her reach.

"Who is this?" Concern laced her mother's voice.

"It's okay, ma'am. My name is Trevor Montgomery. I'm an assistant athletic trainer for Ball State University. Chloe has had a bit of an injury. I've just brought her home from the hospital. Now I'm going to head to the drugstore to pick up her medicine and some crutches."

Her mother gasped. "Is she all right? I'm coming—"

"It's all right, Mrs. Andrews. Chloe will be fine. I'll let her tell you what happened."

Trevor smiled as he handed the phone to Chloe. The look she returned was one that spoke of her desire to cause horrendous pain to his person. He couldn't help but laugh out loud.

Chloe covered the phone with her hand. "I'll get you for this."

He winked. "You don't scare me, Chloe Andrews. In fact, the fire that blazes in your eyes and the grit that fills your spirit do nothing but intrigue me."

three

Chloe hung up the phone after nearly an hour of conversation with her mother. Having attempted to explain to her mom that she would be okay in a few days, Chloe leaned back against the couch cushions knowing it would be a matter of days before Lorma Andrews drove up for a visit. *She'll probably bring Daddy with her.* Chloe closed her eyes. She could hardly bear the thought of seeing her father. Black lung disease had practically taken over his frail body. His coughs hurt her ears. Keeping her distance from him was the only way she had learned to cope with her father's illness.

Chloe jumped when the front door swung open and Liz and Renee bolted inside, with Coach Collins behind them.

"What did they say?" Liz fell to the carpet at Chloe's feet. Renee plopped onto the recliner beside her.

Coach walked over to her. "How are you?"

"I'll be up and at it in a couple days." Chloe tried to smile as a bolt of pain dashed through her ankle as if protesting her words.

"No. She won't."

Chloe looked up to find Trevor shutting the door. He held a bag in one hand and a pair of crutches in the other. Chloe cringed at the sight. There was no way she was using those things for the next few weeks.

"She'll be using these for the next few weeks." Trevor leaned the crutches against the wall. He pulled a container of pills from the bag. "It's been a few hours since your injection at the hospital. My guess is you're needing a couple of these pretty bad about now."

Chloe scowled at him. She would not admit to him, not even for a moment, that she needed something to ease the throbbing in her ankle. She'd rather lie in bed in a cold sweat all night than endure his know-it-all glances.

"How bad is it?" Coach Collins looked at Trevor.

"Third-degree sprain. She'll be out six weeks."

"Six weeks!" Liz, Renee, and Coach exclaimed in unison.

Chloe closed her fists. Everything in her wanted to throttle the trainer. "He's wrong." Chloe spit the words through clenched teeth.

"No. I'm not." He looked at Liz and lifted a couple of pills in the air. "I need to get her a drink of water so she can take these. Where are your glasses?"

"There are some bottles of water in the fridge." Liz didn't take her gaze off Chloe. Disbelief cloaked her and Renee's faces. Coach rubbed his forehead with his forefingers; frustration etched his features. Chloe wanted to crawl under the couch and hide. First she'd spent an hour on the phone with her mother. Now she had to witness her coach and teammates' disappointment.

"Here. Take these." Trevor held out a glass of water and two pills.

She gazed up at him. Desperate to blame him for all that had happened, the sympathy and kindness radiating from his eyes made her want to cry. . .again. She looked away. "I don't want them."

"Take them."

"You do what he tells you." Coach Collins pointed his finger at her. "We need you to do everything he says so you can get better and back out on that field."

Chloe noted the tone in his voice that seemed to say, "Don't worry. All will be fine." Many a player had dug her grave and buried her career with that tone in the past. Though he intended it to sound encouraging, Coach meant he would do whatever necessary to pick up the team and go on—without her. Unbidden tears welled in her eyes. The last thing she wanted was to cry in front of her coach and roommates.

"How about if I help you get settled into your room?"

Chloe looked up at Trevor. He winked. *He knows I'm about to come unglued, and he's getting me out of here.* She nodded and reached her arms around his neck when he bent down to pick her up. *Why is he being nice to me? I've been nasty to him since the moment he came onto the field.*

With ease he carried her into her room and set her on the bed. She combed her hand through the hair that had escaped her ponytail. "Really I need to clean up."

"I know. I just thought you needed to be alone for a minute."

Chloe studied the trainer, the man she'd probably spend a good amount of time with over the next few weeks. Dark stubble had formed on his chin, darker than his hair. It gave him a strong, masculine look and also made his green eyes brighter. There was no question he was attractive, and she definitely enjoyed sparring with him. A smile threatened to form on her lips.

He touched her chin for a moment. "I'll pray for you, Chloe."

She frowned, and her heart fell into her stomach. *Just what I need, more people praying for me.*

ॐ

Trevor tucked the treasured Bible under his arm as he made his way to the church building. It was one of his most prized possessions, and he loved to feel the edges of the duct tape that made up the book's binding. His mother had passed away a little more than twelve years ago, when he was only sixteen, but the notes and written thoughts that filled her Bible made him feel closer to her. He knew her better now than he ever had when she was alive.

He stepped into the building, and his body involuntarily shook from the change in temperature. The cool air-conditioning was a welcome relief from the heat that beat down on him outside. Fall couldn't arrive fast enough.

A vision of a disheveled and pain-filled Chloe sitting on the hospital bed swept through his mind. She had invaded his thoughts quite a bit over the last twenty-four hours. He'd itched to visit her today but decided to give her a day to come to terms with the injury. He couldn't decide whether to smile or shake his head at the unruly yet passionate behavior of the woman. Without a doubt he'd pay her a visit tomorrow. He feared she'd be up trying to walk on her ankle if he didn't keep a close eye on her.

"Hey, Trevor. How's it going?"

Trevor turned at the familiar voice. Joy filled him when one of the men's soccer players walked up to him and shook his hand. "Hello, Matt. I'm glad to see you here again."

"It's been fairly interesting." Matt shrugged his shoulders. "Besides, quite a few attractive women attend this Bible study." He winked.

Trevor grimaced, wanting Matt's reason for coming to church to be more about seeking and less about flirting. *Ah, but, Lord, You say Your word will never come back void. I need to trust You to do a work in him.* "That's true, but what do you think about the Gospel of John?"

Matt furrowed his eyebrows. "I can't decide. I don't know

when he's speaking literally and when it's figurative. The book's keeping my attention, though, which is more than most college professors can do." Matt let out a laugh.

Trevor laughed, as well. "If you ever have any questions, I'd be happy to answer them if I can."

"That'd be great." Matt's gaze followed one of the women who walked past them into the room. He looked back at Trevor. "Hey, I heard there was an injury on the women's team. Chloe Andrews?"

"Yep. She has a third-degree sprain in her ankle. She'll be out six weeks."

Matt shook his head. "Man, that's too bad. She's like their starting center."

"Yep."

"She's kinda cute, too."

A knot formed in Trevor's stomach when Matt wiggled his eyebrows and winked.

"I'll agree she's cute, but as to her ankle, she and I will work on it. We'll get her back on that field as quick as possible." Trevor knew he sounded a bit more possessive than he should have, but the idea of Matt thinking of Chloe more like a package of meat and less like a gifted, spirited young woman grated on Trevor's nerves.

"You'll work wonders." Matt patted Trevor's shoulder. "I might stop at the grocery store on the way home, pick up a few flowers, and take them over to Chloe's apartment." He nudged Trevor with his elbow. "Tell her I'm thinking about her."

Trevor tried not to frown. "That would be. . .nice."

"Guess we'd better go inside."

Trevor watched as Matt walked into the room and sat beside the young woman he'd noticed entering only moments ago. Trevor willed back a scowl as he took a seat in front of

Matt and turned to the scripture the Bible study leader had written on the board.

He tried to focus on the words from the leader, but the woman behind him giggled at something Matt had whispered. Everything in Trevor wanted to turn around and punch Matt in the jaw. How could the guy flirt with one woman when he had plans to go flirt with another right after class? *Why does it even bother me?* He knew the answer. It was Chloe Andrews. The woman had fascinated him in a way no one had before.

But she doesn't know You, Lord.

Trevor's heart sank at the truth of it. He'd never been one to chase after women, wasn't worried about dating in high school or college—until Chloe. Now she was all he could think about. *Lord, this isn't good. How am I going to be her trainer and keep my feelings at bay?*

"Did you hear what the scripture just said?" The leader's voice drew Trevor from his thoughts. "Let me read God's Word again. Jesus said, 'And I will do whatever you ask in my name, so that the Son may bring glory to the Father. You may ask me for anything in my name, and I will do it.'"

Trevor peered down at the text before him and reread what the leader had said.

"Now let me ask you," the leader continued, "do you think this means that if we want a Corvette, Jesus will get us one?"

"Works for me." Someone whooped from behind.

"Sorry, but that's not at all what Jesus is saying." The leader laughed. "Although I'd love a '67 Mustang. Jesus is saying that when we ask for the things He wants, when our requests match His, God will give us what we ask."

"I've been asking God to save my father for ten years," responded a tiny blond a few seats from Trevor. "Surely that is in God's will."

"Yes, it is." The leader nodded his head. "But your father has to decide to accept Christ." He smiled and pointed at her. "You keep praying."

Trevor closed his eyes. *God, I'm falling for a beautiful young woman who I have a hunch doesn't know You. Please draw her to Yourself. May she receive You as Lord of her life, and until she does, keep my heart safe.*

❧

"I *knew* it." Chloe looked through the peephole in the front door. She opened the door. "Mama!" Chloe shifted her weight onto one crutch as she opened the door wide. She hated using the crutches, but when she had tried to put weight on her foot first thing that morning, pain shot through her ankle with such intensity she thought she'd broken it. "Where's Daddy?"

Her mother set her suitcase inside the door and hugged Chloe. "Too sick to come." She pulled away and held her daughter at arm's length. "You have to get down to Otwell and see your father. He's not doing well."

Chloe cleared her throat. Thinking of her father's illness, knowing it would claim him eventually, hurt her to the core of her being. She thought of the many nights all eight children and her mother would sit on the front porch and sing hymns while Daddy played his guitar. It would be only a matter of time before her four older sisters would start fighting over who had the best singing voice. Being the youngest and closest in age to her three older brothers, even though one—her twin—was only ten minutes older than she, Chloe was never included in the fights. *It's silly. I always wanted to fight with them, but they never even acknowledged I was there.*

"Hi, Chloe."

Chloe looked up to find one of her sisters standing in the door. "Kylie, I'm surprised you came." She gazed at her sister's blossoming midsection. "Wow! I didn't even know you were pregnant."

"Well, you don't come down to see us much, and we don't get too many phone calls. Come here, squirt." Kylie stood on tiptoes and enveloped Chloe in her arms.

"I hate that name."

"I guess it really doesn't fit anymore since I have to practically jump up and down, even with you leaning on crutches, to give you a hug."

Chloe grinned. "True."

"Bet you didn't know Ryan and I are adopting two children from Belize also."

"What?"

"Yeah. As soon as the adoption is finalized, I'm really going to be a mommy."

"I can't believe it. You're not still working, are you?"

"No. I won't be able to do that—"

"Girls," their mother interrupted. "Let's talk once we actually get in the apartment and settle Chloe down on the couch."

"Sounds like a plan. My foot is throbbing." Chloe started to make her way to the couch.

"I can't believe you just admitted that."

Chloe turned at the deep voice that spoke behind her. Trevor Montgomery, one of the few men able to do it, peered several inches down at her. She stuck out her tongue at him. "I can't very well admit it to you. You think you're right about everything."

Trevor laughed and extended his hand to her mother. "I'm Trevor Montgomery."

"Lorma Andrews. It's a pleasure to meet you."

Chloe glanced at Kylie as she eased down onto the couch. Kylie pointed toward Trevor then fanned her face and smiled as if to say that Trevor was hot. Chloe couldn't hold back her chuckle when he turned to Kylie and caught her making the gesture. Kylie's face blazed redder than Trevor's when he extended his hand to introduce himself.

"Now that you've met my family, I'm ready for you to fix my ankle." Chloe saved her sister from having to say anything to Trevor.

"I won't be able to fix it." He walked over to her, bent down, and pulled the Velcro from her air cast. After taking it off, he touched both sides of her foot. She flinched despite her attempt not to. "It's still quite swollen." He shook his head. "You're just going to have to rest it for a few weeks. You are still putting ice on it, right?"

Nodding, Chloe's heart fluttered when his fingers stayed just above her ankle. He rubbed the swollen spots, asking if any hurt. Heat filled her at the tenderness of his touch, and Chloe wondered if her face blazed as her sister's had only moments before. Glancing at Kylie and noting the smirk draping her features, Chloe knew her face glowed just as she feared. "A few weeks is too long." She pulled her foot away from him.

Trevor rolled his eyes. "Yes, but if you want to get back in the game, you have to do as I say."

Chloe's flutters flitted away at the tone of his voice. They were replaced by hot anger streaming through her veins. He was not her boss, her daddy, or her coach. He did not know everything. Her body would heal quickly, faster than he could ever imagine. She'd show him!

"So have you had any visitors?" His gaze scanned her

apartment until he spotted the vase of flowers on the dining room table. "Someone sent you flowers?"

Chloe shifted in her seat. "Yes. Matt stopped by last night. You probably know him. He plays on the—"

"Matt Ellis."

The scowl that filled his expression piqued Chloe's curiosity. Why would Trevor care if Matt brought her flowers? If she didn't know better, she'd believe Trevor was jealous. *That's ridiculous. He's made it perfectly clear that I am nothing more than an aggravation to him.*

Trevor's scowl disappeared, and he looked at her mother. "How long are you staying?"

"Just a couple of days."

"That's too bad." He stared at Chloe and seemed to force a smile. "It's going to be hard to make her stay off her ankle."

"I can try to stay a bit longer," her mother answered. "It's just that—"

"No. You need to go home to Daddy." She turned to Trevor. "My father was a coal miner for years. Now he's very ill with black lung disease."

Trevor stood and touched her mother's shoulder. "I'm sorry. My mom died from breast cancer when I was sixteen. It was the hardest thing I've ever experienced."

Chloe studied Trevor. She couldn't imagine the pain he must have felt. Yet he hadn't become bitter by it. He didn't seem to have distanced himself from people. Chloe could hardly even visit her father. He was alive, yet she didn't have the courage to go visit him because it hurt *her* too much. Shame filled her heart. As soon as she could, she would make the trip to Otwell to see her daddy.

"What's his name?" Trevor's question interrupted her thoughts.

"Richard Andrews."

"If it's all right, I'll add him to my church's prayer list. I'll be sure to pray for him every day, as well."

A tear slipped down her mother's cheek. She brushed it away with the back of her hand. "That would be wonderful. Thank you."

Chloe watched as Trevor bent down and gave her mother a quick hug. The man was perfect. Except for the "praying" thing. She'd had her fill of praying growing up in the Andrews home. In her opinion, not a whole lot had come of it.

four

"Why do you keep asking me about Trevor Montgomery?" Chloe dropped her crutches against the bleachers at the soccer field and sat down. She helped coach a local soccer team of young girls. Most of the teens were already on the field dribbling their soccer balls around each other before practice started.

Kylie lowered onto the bleacher with a loud sigh. "I don't know. He's kinda cute, super attentive to you"—she leaned closer to Chloe—"and he's a Christian."

"Humph." Chloe bent over to see if her ankle had started to swell again. Yesterday it had almost looked normal, but when she tried to make her way without crutches to the bathroom in the middle of the night, the ankle swelled again. *A whole week's passed, and it's still swollen.* She growled and hit the bleacher.

"It's not going to heal unless you listen to your trainer. . . your very handsome trainer."

Chloe glared at her sister. "I don't care that he's cute. Don't care that he's attentive. And I definitely don't care that he's a Christian."

"What's that supposed to mean?"

"Nothing. I'm just not interested. Okay, Kylie?"

"Fine." Kylie stood. "I'm going to the bathroom. Could you do me a favor?"

"What?" Chloe snapped.

"By the time I get back, decide to be nice. I'm sorry about

32

your ankle, but I'm tired of listening to your pouty, poor-me attitude." She pointed her finger at Chloe. "And you need to shape up in the way you're treating Mama. You were raised to be respectful and kind, but you've acted like a spoiled brat since we got here. We're leaving tomorrow, and there's no telling when you'll decide to grace us with your presence again. Act like you're happy your mother has come to see you." She turned and stomped toward the restroom.

Chloe rested her elbows on her knees and looked at the ground. She had acted like a jerk the last few days. But it was her ankle. If it weren't for her injury, she'd be her normal, happy self. *"No matter my circumstance, I have learned to be content."* Her father's echoing of the apostle Paul's words filled her mind. He'd spoken of contentment several times when she saw him last. He'd coughed and hacked, and his face had scrunched up in obvious pain each time he said it. She didn't understand how he could talk of peace no matter what.

Her heart felt heavy, and she closed her eyes. *What am I missing?* Her ankle started to throb, and she wished to yank out the pain and throw it away from her.

"Hey, Coach." Interrupting her thoughts, one of the teen girls plopped down beside her. "What happened to your foot?"

"Sprained my ankle."

"Is that all? I sprained my ankle once, and Mom told me to walk it off. I did, and it was fine."

Chloe frowned. "I wish mine were that easy."

The girl sighed. "I guess you won't be able to practice with us today."

"Only from the sidelines."

"That stinks."

"Believe me." Chloe tightened the Velcro on her air cast. "I totally agree."

❧

Trevor stayed close to Chloe as she walked on crutches toward the soccer field. Two weeks had passed since her injury, and her ankle wasn't healing well. It still swelled when she tried to walk on it. She'd been silent on the drive over. He knew watching the first game of the season, her senior season, was almost more than she could bear. The team and coaches had gone onto the field, warming up before the game. He and Chloe took their seats beside the team's bench. Glancing at her, his heart constricted at the longing that showed on her face.

What can I say to make her feel better? He peeked at her profile. Strands of long hair escaped her ponytail and kissed her cheek. Long dark lashes fanned from eyes that focused with intensity on the happenings on the field. Her straight posture exuded a confidence unlike that of many women he knew; yet he had seen the vulnerability she tried so hard to hide. She was a force to reckon with. A pillar of strength for her team. A pillar built on sand that had begun to shift.

Ah, Jesus, I'm intrigued with her. I can't deny it. I want to know her better. More. He shook the admission away. Being honest about his feelings was one thing, but succumbing to them was quite another. He could think of Chloe only as a soccer player in need of his expertise. *Unless she gives her life over to You.*

No. He couldn't think like that, couldn't entertain considering a relationship with her. Sure, he would pray for her, and one day she might receive Christ into her heart. But he'd known far too many Christians who found themselves in wrong relationships because they'd banked on the hope that one day their other half would accept Christ.

"Chloe?"

"What?"

Her response was quick, almost harsh, and Trevor nearly laughed out loud. He was thinking of relationships, and Chloe had given him every reason to believe she found him to be the most aggravating, annoying man on the planet. *Why would I want to mess with the woman anyway? She's completely difficult.*

Chloe looked at him. "I'm sorry I snapped at you." The blue in her eyes shimmered with the threat of tears. "This is harder than I expected."

"I know." Desire to wrap his arm around her shoulder and fear she would be offended by the gesture warred within him. He nudged her arm with his elbow. "How was your visit with your mom and sister?"

"Good. I guess. They left a couple of days ago." She nodded her head then looked away from him. "I need to go see my dad."

"I'd be happy to take you to see him." Trevor leaned back, surprised at his offer. "I mean, if you want me to."

"Why would you do that?" Her icy blue eyes pierced him.

Why would he? Because he was attracted to her? Because he wanted to know her better? Because he wanted to share his faith with her? A good Christian would say the latter, but Trevor knew his heart. He was treading on ultra-thin ice, and if he wasn't careful, he'd have more than slipping to worry about. A dip in freezing water was more likely. "To help you out, I guess."

She nodded as the team raced from the field with only minutes before the game was to begin. "I may take you up on that."

Coach Collins flopped down beside him. He pointed to Chloe, who was talking to a teammate. "How's my girl?"

Beautiful. Wonderful. A gem that needs the mire washed away from it by the pure blood of Jesus. None of those estimations was what her coach wanted to hear. "Doing all right."

"How much longer?"

"I don't know. I hoped to begin physical therapy by now, but her ankle is still swelling." He shrugged his shoulder. "Maybe five weeks. If she listens to me."

Coach Collins frowned. "Is she not doing what she's supposed to?"

"I have a feeling she's tried to walk on it a few times, but true injury has a way of forcing us to believe it's there."

"Molly's taking her place for now. She's been doing well in practice. We'll see how the game goes. We won the coin toss."

The coach stood and huddled with the girls. After he gave a quick pep talk, the team parted, and the starters ran out on the field. The referee blew the whistle, and Molly took control of the ball, dribbled past the fullbacks, and kicked it into the goal. The fans went wild with excitement, as did the players.

"Did you see that?" Coach clapped his hands. "I've never seen a gal take control and score so quickly. Not in a college game anyway." He cupped his hand around his mouth. "Great job, Molly!"

Trevor glanced at Chloe. Though a smile bowed her lips and her hands met and separated in a clap, fear filled her eyes. Molly had taken her spot.

❧

Molly has my spot. She glared at the air cast wrapped around her ankle. *It has to heal. Now! Yesterday!* Peeking at Coach, she watched as he jumped up and down and his fists pumped the air. Her hands grew sticky as a cold sweat covered her skin. Her senior year. Her last season to play for the Cardinals.

And she sat on the bench like a second-string player. *At least a second-string player has the chance of getting in the game. I don't.*

She peered out at the partially filled stands. It would have been nice to see her mama and daddy out there. A sudden wave of memories cascaded through her mind. It was her last game of high school. The whole family had come to support her. Each with their faces painted green and yellow—the school's colors. Even her youngest nephew, only eight months at the time, had paint smudged on his cheeks. All of them had her number, lucky thirteen, painted in deepest gold on the front of their green sweatshirts. The October night had been bitter cold, even for Indiana. But they'd come. All of them. To support her. She'd not only scored every goal for her team, but also been awarded a full-ride scholarship to Ball State University.

She snapped from the memory. For the first time in four years, she didn't feel able to control a soccer field. Didn't feel capable of putting an opposing player in her place with amazing dribbling skills. She watched as Molly took control of the ball again. For once someone was better than she was. Chloe longed for her family.

She needed someone besides herself.

five

Chloe checked her reflection in the Muncie Mall restroom mirror. She raked her fingers through her hair, still surprised at how much she liked her new haircut. The long layers the stylist had trimmed into her tresses that fell well past her shoulders gave life to her normally plain style. Opening her purse, she fished out her melon-colored lip gloss and applied it to her lips. The subtle color complemented her sleeveless sweater perfectly. It was an unusual occasion that Chloe felt pretty or even feminine. This happened to be one of those rare moments.

And she liked it.

After shoving the lip gloss back in her purse, she snapped the bag shut and lifted the long skinny strap over her head, allowing the strap to rest on her left shoulder and the purse to rest at her right hip. Though more of a sporty look, it was the only way she could carry it and use her crutches. Her moment of femininity rushed away as she leaned on the crutches.

She felt anything but pretty using them.

Remembering a friend from high school who'd had to use a walker because of cerebral palsy, a flash of shame shot through her. Chloe had always deemed Rebecca beautiful, as had everyone in her class. *It's just hard when you're not used to them*, she told herself. She stood up, putting her weight on her good foot, and lifted her arm above her head. Walking from shop to shop had left a large raw spot under both of her arms. Each step was agony, but there was no way Chloe would admit it to her friends.

"You about ready?"

Chloe dropped her arm when Liz stepped into the rest area. "Yep." She leaned into her crutches and gritted against the pain as she followed her friend.

"Renee wants to stop by her favorite department store. There's a jacket she said she's been eyeballing for weeks. With all the sales going on today. . ."

The raw spots took precedence over Liz's babbling. Chloe tried to listen. She ground her teeth with each step she took, the pain was so intense. This was their shopping trip to celebrate their first victory of the year, and she didn't know how she would make it through several more hours. She couldn't fathom enduring the pain, but she couldn't admit defeat, either.

"Chloe, I'm going to grab a pretzel. Want to go with me?"

Glancing at the owner of the voice, Chloe was surprised to see it was Molly, the gal who'd taken her position on the soccer field. Chloe had given the younger girl the cold shoulder all day, and in truth Chloe had zero desire to hang out with the sophomore. She planned to earn her spot back as soon as her ankle decided to cooperate, but the chance to sit a moment or two was too enticing to pass up. "Sure."

After making her way to the stand, Chloe ordered a pretzel with chocolate dip and a large soda. She grabbed her pretzel and realized she wouldn't be able to carry her dip and drink, as well. She scowled at her crutches. She hated them. Everything in her wanted to throw them through the glass display window before her.

"I've got it. You go sit."

Chloe looked at Molly. The girl's expression was tender, compassionate, and completely infuriating. But what choice did Chloe have? "Thanks." She forced a smile. Why had she agreed to this outing in the first place? Trevor would kill her if he found out. And her ankle throbbed nearly as much as it had the first day.

Flopping onto one of the benches in the center of the mall, she pushed a fake leaf from the potted tree beside her away from her face. She laid the crutches against the pot and leaned back on the bench, allowing a soft sigh to escape her lips.

"They're no fun, huh?" Molly sat beside her and scooped Chloe's food from the tray then handed it to her.

"What?"

"Your crutches."

Chloe shrugged. "I'll live."

"Use baby powder."

"What?"

"On your arms. It doesn't take away all the pain, but the powder keeps you from getting too raw."

Chloe stared at her pretzel. Obviously her attempt at showing no pain had failed. She took a drink, fighting the emotions welling inside her. Chloe Andrews had always been the strong one. The one who could outplay everyone, even her brothers' friends. Now she had to use baby powder for her chafed armpits. The humiliation was unbearable.

"You know I had to sit out my entire senior year in high school. Broke my foot in two places." Molly's voice was soft. She picked off a piece of pretzel and popped it into her mouth.

Chloe turned and took in the girl sitting beside her. Molly, though several inches shorter than Chloe, was a powerhouse. Even sitting casually, the muscles in her arms and legs flexed slightly with each move she made. Her short, apparently dyed blond hair was cut so she had straight bangs parted to one side and blunt spikes around the back of her head. The mere sight of Molly screamed athlete. Chloe tilted her head.

Or punk rocker. But Molly's dark chocolate eyes were kind and honest. Her gaze extended help and friendship, as did her smile.

Chloe swallowed, realizing she'd never once extended an offer of help to the sophomore, never even asked how practice was going or if transferring was working out for her. Her feelings of leadership waned as she inwardly admitted she hadn't been the leader she should have been to this teammate and probably others. "How'd you break it? Driving in on a goalie?"

A twinge of pink dotted Molly's cheeks, and her lips bowed up. "Actually. . ." She pulled off another piece of pretzel and dipped it in her nacho cheese before taking the bite. "It's a bit embarrassing." Swallowing, she feigned choking and shoved her straw into her mouth.

Chloe laughed and smacked Molly's back. "Come on. You gotta tell me now."

"Okay, okay." Molly set her cup on the floor. She brushed crumbs from her legs. "My little brother's skateboard was sitting in the driveway one day. I'd seen him do flips and whatnot on the thing and wondered what it would be like to try to stand on a board on wheels." Molly stopped, shook her head, and stared at the ceiling.

Chloe felt her eyebrows lift as her mouth opened. This was the last thing she expected. "And. . ." She motioned for Molly to go on.

"And our driveway is on a bit of a hill. Which I hadn't considered when I jumped on the board." She clapped her hands. "The thing shot down the driveway so fast I hit the curb at the bottom, went flying through the air, and landed in the road."

"You're lucky you weren't hurt worse."

"My mom saw the whole thing. She laughed so hard, wishing she'd had the camcorder. She felt sure we'd have won the grand prize on *America's Funniest Home Videos*."

"But your foot."

Molly nodded. "Yeah. It was tough. I was captain of our team. Felt like I'd let them down." She shrugged her shoulders. "In a funny way it was the best thing that ever happened to me. I realized the team was made up of more people than just me. We even came in second in the state that year."

Chloe gripped her drink. Condensation cooled her fingertips. She put the cup down and wiped her hands on her capris. How could anyone believe an injury to be a good thing? Chloe surely didn't. She knew it took more than just her to make up the team, but she was still a valuable part of it, a needed component. Glancing at Molly, her heart and mind warred within her. Molly had taken Chloe's spot. Maybe this kindness and the pep talk were nothing more than a facade, a way of making Chloe want to give in to the injury and allow Molly to steal her place. *Time will tell if Molly is really just playing me.*

A contemporary Christian song suddenly blared from Molly's purse. She scooped her cell phone from it, pushed TALK, and held it to her ear. Chloe only half listened to the one-sided conversation as she watched people walk on strong, healthy legs back and forth in front of her. Her mind replayed every encounter she'd had with Molly, trying to decipher if she should trust the sophomore.

"The girls are heading this way." Molly interrupted her thoughts. She put her phone back in her purse. "They shouldn't be here for another twenty minutes. Maybe we could call someone to come pick you up."

Chloe frowned. "What are you talking about? I'm going home with you guys."

"Some of the guys from the men's soccer team are with them."

"So?"

"Trevor, too."

Chloe lifted her eyebrows as a wave of panic washed through her. "Oh no."

Molly bobbed her head and grabbed the pretzel from Chloe's hands and picked up the drinks from the floor. Standing, she shoved them into the trash and helped Chloe to her feet. "If we move quick, he'll never know you were here."

"You knew I wasn't supposed to come."

"Oh yeah."

"You didn't say anything."

"I understood."

"Now you're helping me out of here so my trainer doesn't go ballistic on me."

"Well, yeah."

Chloe let out a long breath. "You really want to help me, don't you?"

"I'd like to think we're friends." Molly turned to face her. "At the very least, we're teammates."

Chloe touched Molly's arm, realizing the sophomore was a teammate in the truest of ways. She wanted what was best for Chloe. Molly was different from most of the girls. Though it pained her to admit it, she was different from Chloe, as well. *I can change all that. I can become the person who cares about what's best for others.* "Definitely friends."

"Who can we call?" Molly pulled out her phone again.

"I don't know. Both of my roommates are here." She followed Molly's much-too-quick steps toward an exit. "How 'bout Sarah? She's not here."

"Good idea. She's back at practice after her knee surgery, so she's definitely got to be able to drive again." Molly scrolled through telephone numbers on her cell phone as Chloe made her way past another store.

"Tell her I'll sit right out front—" Chloe ran into what felt like a brick wall. She gasped and peered up at the man. "I'm so sorry. I'm. . ."

The man's brows met in a furrowed frown, and his gaze settled on her foot. He crossed his arms in front of his chest. "Imagine seeing you here." Trevor's voice dripped with sarcasm.

"Busted."

&

"Well, I. . ."

Trevor watched as Chloe's gaze darted from him to the displays around him. Her lips pursed together, and he knew she was trying to conjure a good explanation for being at the mall when she should be resting. In his experience, athletes were notorious for pushing their injuries too far. In the limited time he'd known Chloe, he'd recognized she was an athlete. He'd have to keep reminding her of her need for rest. *I'll probably have to padlock her door and physically sit on her to get her to stay off that ankle.* Frustration seethed through every inch of his marrow. The woman would never heal if she didn't heed his instructions.

Molly shut her cell phone. "Guess I don't need to call Sarah."

Chloe's cheeks blazed red. "Guess not."

"Why were you calling Sarah?" Trevor lifted his eyebrows and glanced from one girl to the other. "Trying to make an escape from the big, bad Trevor?"

"Something like that." Molly looked away.

"Of course I am an adult. Capable of making my own choices," Chloe mumbled.

"Yes, but if you want back on that field—"

"Hey, you guys." Liz's voice interrupted Trevor. "I'm so glad we caught up with you." Liz put her arm around Molly. The majority of the men's and women's soccer teams huddled in a mass in the center of the mall. "Matt wants to go to Pizza King."

"Matt hungry." Matt wiggled his eyebrows and rubbed his stomach.

"Yum." Molly nodded. "I love Pizza King. We don't have any where I'm from."

"Where are you from? The moon?" Matt elbowed Trevor and snorted.

"No, Kentucky. But I love Pizza King so much I may graduate and start my own chain back home."

"I love their barbecue sauce supreme." Chloe shifted her crutches, and Trevor noted the raw spots under her arms. Not only did the woman not need to be waltzing around the mall, but he also would have thought she'd have enough sense to wear more than a sleeveless sweater to pad her arms. Even though the color did look pretty on her.

"Let's go, then." Matt moved closer to Chloe. "You look gorgeous."

Her skin turned pink, and she looked at the ground. "Thanks."

Trevor's heart raced, and his hands clammed up. Couldn't she see? Didn't she know Matt was a shameless flirt? But there she was acting flattered by such a shallow comment. *Even if I was thinking the same thing. Why didn't I say it first?*

The group had already made its way out of the mall. Only Matt and Trevor had lingered with Chloe. Searching for something, anything, to say, Trevor shoved his hand in his jeans pocket, yanked out his car keys, and gripped them. His blood boiled at the very thought of Matt going after Chloe.

"You want to ride over with me?" Matt's voice dripped with sweetness, making Trevor want to punch the younger man in the nose.

Chloe giggled and nodded her head as Trevor shook his. He couldn't believe Chloe was gullible enough to fall for the infamous flirt's charms. Jealousy and disbelief filled him as his mind raced for a way to keep Chloe from Matt.

"Hurry up!" one of the men's soccer players yelled to Matt as they walked into the parking lot. "The doors are locked." Two other players gestured to Matt, as well.

Trevor's grin spread over his face, his cheeks almost pained at the fullness of it. "Looks like your car's loaded. Chloe can ride with me."

Matt glanced at him. "Unless you want to do a buddy a favor and give those guys a ride."

Trevor shrugged. "Can't do it. I haven't cleaned my physical therapy equipment out of the backseat of my car yet."

"Fine. See ya at Pizza King, Chloe." Matt walked away from them.

Trevor unlocked his car and opened the door for Chloe. He took her crutches from her and laid them in the backseat on top of all his stuff. *I should have cleaned this mess weeks ago.* He inwardly chuckled. *Sometimes procrastination pays off.* He walked around the car and settled into the driver's seat.

"Go ahead and let me have it."

He glanced at Chloe as she buckled her seat belt then stared out the windshield. To her, he was the constant naysayer, the antagonist, the enemy. How he wished they had met under different circumstances. And that she was a Christian. *Oh Lord, I should have found a way to let her ride with Matt. I can't pursue her.*

"Go ahead. I'm waiting."

Trevor started the car. "I wasn't going to say anything to you about your ankle." He pulled out of the mall parking lot and into traffic. "I did notice you have a raw spot under your arm. . . ."

"Ugh." She slapped her leg. "I wish I'd never worn this sweater. It was new, and I liked the color. . . ."

"It looks nice on you."

She looked out her window. "Thanks."

"I have some ointment that might help your arms."

‌

Chloe listened to the chatter around the table at Pizza King. Matt kept *accidentally* bumping into her foot under the table. She was beginning to believe it was his adolescent way of flirting with her. Evidently he didn't remember she had a severely sprained ankle and each little tap hurt like crazy.

She bit into her pizza and glanced at Molly and Trevor. Whatever they were discussing must have been interesting, because they seemed completely enthralled with what the other had to say. Both had surprised her on this outing. Molly had been kind to Chloe when she had nothing to gain, when Chloe had been anything but kind to her. Trevor also didn't lay into her for not listening to his instructions. He'd pointedly, without reservation or confusion, told her to stay completely off her ankle. She didn't heed him, and he didn't get mad. *But why?*

Deep in her heart she knew the answer. Molly and Trevor were like the Andrews clan. The whole lot of them. They probably loved God. Probably had a relationship with Him. Talked to Him as if He was present and could do something in their lives.

As if He could provide money when none was there.

As if He could heal ankles that had been injured.

As if He could take black lung out of a man.

Sure, God had provided money for her family each time they needed it. Even allowed her sister Kylie to marry a wealthy husband who loved to help the family. And Chloe's ankle, given time, would heal.

But what about Daddy, God? He's not going to heal. He's going to die from black lung. A man who has been nothing but good all his life, who has followed You and cared for his family. A wonderful, wonderful man. How is that fair?

A single tear slipped down her cheek. She swiped it away, realizing she still sat at the table with her friends around her. Gazing at each face, she sighed. She didn't think anyone had seen her moment of weakness. No one except Trevor. A puzzled look overtook his features as he silently mouthed, *Are you okay?*

She smiled and nodded then grabbed her soda and took a long drink.

"I have an idea." Matt clinked his fork against the side of his red plastic cup. "Let's go putt-putt golfing."

"That sounds great." Liz motioned for the waitress.

Dread filled Chloe's heart. Her arms were throbbing, more so than her ankle. She wanted nothing more than to go back to the apartment, draw a hot bath, and soak for an hour or more.

"Sorry, you guys, but I'm beat. I have some equipment I need to give Chloe for when we start our therapy sessions." Trevor looked at Chloe and winked. "If it's all right with you, I'll take you home and give it to you now."

"That would be fine." Relief swept through her. Whether he realized it or not, Trevor had just acted like an angel sent from God. She studied him a moment, watching as he walked around the table, picked up her crutches, and helped her to her feet. Maybe he wasn't an angel but a messenger from God. With the same story she'd heard all her life. The one her whole family put their complete faith in.

Everyone except Chloe.

six

Trevor jingled his keys as he strode up the sidewalk to Chloe's apartment. Something had changed with Chloe since their outing at the mall and Pizza King two weeks earlier. She'd begun heeding his instructions and had even started some rehabilitative exercises a week ago. So far her ankle had held up well, but he knew the fact that she'd already missed several games weighed heavily on her heart. *Which is why I have a surprise for her today.*

In truth Liz and Renee had come up with the surprise. He'd received an unexpected visit from the twosome four days ago. At first he'd been hesitant to go along with their plan, especially since both would be visiting their families and couldn't go with him. But when they'd used Liz's cell phone to call Chloe's mom, the older woman had expressed such excitement that Trevor simply couldn't deny the request.

A flash of uncertainty zipped through him. *Chloe may not be as gung ho as her mother and friends think she'll be.* He shook his head, squelching the thought. Biting the inside of his lip, he suppressed his anxiety as he knocked on the door. She opened it, and he noticed her faded jean shorts and red university shirt. He had to admit she looked nice. Sure, her attire fit the mission she thought they had—rehabilitating her ankle—but he couldn't deny her natural appearance attracted him.

"You look cute." The thought slipped from his lips.

"Yeah, right. You're lucky I showered." She snorted and

punched his arm. "If my trainer wasn't such a slave driver, I wouldn't be such a sweaty mess after one of his sessions."

He glanced down at her ankle, which still sported an air cast for protection, but she carried no crutches to chafe her arms. "True, but you're healing nicely."

She nodded as she shut the front door and started down the sidewalk. "But I'm dying to get back on that field."

"I know. You'll get there."

Trevor opened the car door for her then walked around to the driver's side. Slipping in, he buckled his seat belt, started the car, and drove toward Interstate 69. He tried to pay attention to what Chloe was saying but couldn't stop wincing every time she diverted her attention to the scenery around them. *This is supposed to be a surprise, but I know she'll figure it out. At any moment I'm going to hear it.* So far she hadn't caught on that Trevor was heading in a completely different direction from the university. Turning onto I-69 South, though, he noted that Chloe's eyebrows were furrowed.

"This isn't the way to the university. Where are we going?"

"Not to the university." Trevor tried to hold back the smile that threatened to overtake his mouth.

"Look—we don't know each other that well." She played with the seat belt buckle. "You have to tell me where we're going, or I'm jumping out of this car."

Trevor threw back his head and laughed. "You've got to be kidding." He glanced at Chloe and saw nothing but determination etching her features. Growing serious, he cleared his throat. "Chloe, I wouldn't hurt you."

"I know you won't hurt me, but I don't like not knowing what's going on."

Trevor nodded his head. The vulnerability thing. He should have thought of that before he let himself be bamboozled into taking her on this trip. He'd hoped to get a good ways toward Otwell before revealing the mystery, but he should have known Chloe would never go for it. "We're heading to Otwell."

She frowned. "Otwell? Why?"

"To visit your parents."

"My parents? But we have practice tonight. I can't miss. It's over three hours one way, and—"

"I already told Coach we wouldn't be at practice. Chloe, it's Labor Day. It's an optional, workout practice. You know that. Besides, you can't practice with them yet."

"Told Coach? Told Coach! Trevor, I want to get my spot back. How am I going to do that if I miss practices? Even optional practices? What if I had a paper due Tuesday that I needed to work on tonight—or a test?"

"School just started a couple of weeks ago."

"So? I could have some really picky, crazy professor. You can't just do these things without asking me."

"We wanted to surprise you. Liz and Renee thought this trip would be good for you." Frustration welled within him. Her friends had been wrong, so very wrong.

"Liz and Renee? What do they—?"

"They came to my office a few days ago. They thought a trip to see your family would get your mind off your ankle."

Chloe crossed her arms in front of her. "What do they know? You should have asked me. Just turn around. Go back."

"I can't. Your family knows we're coming."

"Great." Chloe leaned back in the seat and let out a sigh. "Thanks for the surprise." Her tone was laced with sarcasm.

Trevor grabbed a piece of gum from his car's console. After unwrapping the paper, he popped it into his mouth. It was going to be a long drive down there and probably an even longer one on the way home. He glanced at Chloe, whose body posture reminded him of a two-year-old's. *I've got it. No more surprises.*

✦

Chloe flinched as each one of her family members hugged her when she walked through the door. They were an over-whelming crew. Her oldest sisters, Sabrina and Natalie, had three children each. Kylie was pregnant with her first, with two more to come from Belize. Dalton had five children; Amanda had seven. Gideon, Cameron, her twin brother, and Chloe, the babies of the family, were the only ones without a passel running around their feet. Somehow the whole lot of them, spouses included, fit inside Mama and Daddy's small three-bedroom, one-bath house.

"Let me through." Chloe watched as her mother gingerly pushed her way past children and grandchildren to get to her youngest daughter. Her mother threw her arms around Chloe, squeezing with more strength than Chloe would have believed her mom could muster. "It's good to see you, dear. Your father will be so happy you've come."

Dread filled Chloe as her mother guided her toward her parents' bedroom. The room seemed to fog over when she walked into it, and Chloe felt as if she had stepped into another world. She couldn't possibly be inside her parents' bedroom to see her daddy. At any moment he would jump out through the closet door and lift her up over his shoulders and twirl her around as he had when she was little. He was still strong. Still healthy. He had to be.

She could hear her brothers and Trevor talking about football teams in the background. The sounds of children playing and her sisters chattering echoed around her. Steam gurgled from the door. The fog had been real, seeping from the oversized humidifier resting in the corner. A clear cord connected a large machine to the near lifeless figure that raised its hand from the mass of blankets and pillows covering the bed. The hand motioned her forward. Tears clouded her eyes, and she took slow, small steps toward it.

Peering down at the figure—her daddy—the dam broke, and tears streamed down her cheeks. He hadn't looked like this the last time she saw him. He'd been sitting up, eating snacks in bed and telling jokes. Sure, the same tube had stretched from his nose to the machine, but he'd been able to move around. It was obvious that was no longer possible.

A slight smile bowed his lips as he reached for her hand. "Chloe." The word cost him, and he sucked in several quick breaths.

"Oh, Daddy." Chloe allowed the pain and fear to fill her heart. Gently she enveloped her precious father in her arms and drew in the smell of him—still the same as when she was a girl, only now mingled with sickness. Memories of him strong and happy flooded her. Sitting on the front porch singing. Passing the baseball with her brothers. Kicking the soccer ball. Fishing. Helping Mama in the kitchen and stealing kisses when he thought the kids weren't looking.

Hardly any of him was left. Releasing her hug, she peered into his deep blue eyes. No. All of him was there. Just in a different form. A form she didn't like and didn't want to see. Dipping her head, she kissed his forehead then grabbed his hand in hers. "How long has it been since I've seen you, Daddy?"

"Almost nine months." Her mother's soft voice answered for him. "He's missed you. We all have."

"I'm sorry." Regret overcame her, and renewed tears filled her eyes. "So sorry."

"You're here now." Her mother's gentle hand rested on her shoulder. "Let me show you something." She picked up a photo album from the nightstand beside her father. "Your brothers and sisters and I have been keeping an album of you. Your daddy loves to look at it. Each and every night."

Chloe peered at the album then back at her father. His eyes shone with happiness. He raised his eyebrows and nodded his head. "I think he wants me to look at it."

"He probably wants to look at it with you."

Chloe took the album from her mother's grasp and watched as she walked out of the room. Chloe opened to the first page. It was a picture of her soccer team. The names of all her teammates were written in calligraphy underneath the picture. The next page was a photo of her dribbling the ball around an opposing player. As she flipped through more pages, she watched as her father's smile grew and his eyes glistened. She turned the page, and her father pointed to a picture of Chloe celebrating after scoring the winning goal.

"So proud." He whispered the words as he reached over and touched Chloe's cheek.

"I've missed you, Daddy." He smiled and nodded as she grabbed his hand in her own. "It hurts to see you sick. You've got to get well."

Compassion filled his expression as he slowly shook his head. He pointed and gazed at the ceiling. "Jesus."

"No, Daddy." Chloe's eyes widened. "We want you here. We. . .I need you."

He tightened his hold on her hand ever so slightly but still weakly. "No." He swallowed and pointed to the ceiling again. Unblinking, he stared into her eyes. A sweetness cloaked his expression. An excitement, as well. "Jesus."

Chloe nodded as an unknown peace filled her. He was

ready, and she had to be. "Okay, Daddy." Placing the album back on the nightstand, Chloe pulled the chair as close to her father's bed as she could get it. "How 'bout we just spend some time together?"

The hours moved too quickly as Chloe shared one story, thought, or question after another with her father. When Mama walked into the room and said it was time for supper, Chloe never would have imagined she'd been talking for so long. She looked at her watch. "I can't believe it's this late."

Her mother's eyes looked sad. "Yes, I know you'll have to be leaving soon." She patted her husband's hand then gazed at Chloe. "We've missed you so much."

"I'll be back. I won't stay gone again." She leaned close to her father and kissed his sunken cheek. "In a week. I'll be back in a week."

Daddy nodded and whispered, "Love you." He closed his eyes and took long breaths.

"He's plumb tuckered out." Mama fluffed the pillows around him then turned and wrapped her arms around Chloe. "We'd love to see you again next week."

Chloe followed her mother out of the bedroom. Glancing around the room, she was surprised to find everyone gone. Only Trevor sat on the living room sofa flipping through one of her mother's landscaping magazines. A giggle welled in her throat. "Plant many flowers?"

Trevor looked up at her and smiled. "One day I might."

"I'd love to see you use those hands for something besides killing my ankle."

"Hmm." A playful glimmer flashed in his eyes. "My hands might not hurt that ankle if its owner followed instructions."

Chloe planted her hands on her hips, feigning insult. "I'll have you know I've been doing just as my trainer directed."

"Okay, you two." Mama swatted the air. "It's almost seven, and you have well over three hours of driving ahead of you." She crossed to the table and picked up a plastic bag. "I've packed enough food for both of you. You shouldn't have to stop for anything, except maybe gas." She turned toward Chloe. "Go ahead and use the restroom before you leave."

"Mother!" Chloe's mouth dropped as a low chuckle sounded from Trevor.

Mama winked at her. "I was going to tell Trevor the same."

Within moments the twosome had said their good-byes, settled in the car, and headed down the road. Overwhelming emotion swelled within Chloe. She felt happy and sad, thankful and hurt all at the same time. Staring out the window, she studied the passing cornfields and cow pastures. Trevor didn't offer conversation, and she appreciated his thoughtfulness. Fatigue weighed her down, and she found her eyelids begging to close. Maybe shutting them just a moment wouldn't hurt.

"We're here."

Chloe jumped at Trevor's whispered words and light touch. She blinked and wiped her eyes until they focused on her apartment door. "That was fast."

"You slept a good ways."

She felt the heat in her cheeks. "Sorry."

"Don't be sorry."

She opened the car door and fumbled with her seat belt. Glancing back at Trevor, she peered into his eyes, hoping he could see to the depths of her being. "Thanks. . .I mean, I. . ." She picked at a thread that hung from her shirt. "I'm really glad you took me. Thank you."

"You're welcome." The sweet sincerity in his gaze made her heart feel warm. "Anytime. I'll walk you to the door."

"No. You don't need to."

"I don't mind."

"No. It's not like we're on a date."

He lifted his eyebrows and seemed to hold his breath as a blank expression washed over his features. Her comment obviously surprised him. But why? Perplexed, Chloe stepped out of the car and started to shut the door.

"Chloe. Wait." He reached into the backseat. "Don't forget your purse. Your mom found it."

"I didn't take my purse."

"You didn't?" He gazed at the object in his hand.

"Let me see it." She fumbled through the contents for a wallet of some kind. A salvation tract fell out. Chloe reached down and picked it up before searching more. Finding the wallet, she opened it. "It's Natalie's. I bet she's looking for it everywhere. I'm going inside to call her. I'll have to overnight it, but what if something happened or it was lost? I'm sure all her credit cards. . .I'll have to get this back down there to her."

"I will be happy to take you if she can wait until the weekend."

"You would?"

"Sure. I loved your family. They're a lot of fun."

Chloe smiled. They were definitely a lot of things, and she had to admit fun was one of them. "I'd appreciate that. I'll see you tomorrow for my therapy session." She furrowed her brows. "I *am* having therapy tomorrow, right?"

"Yep. I'll see you tomorrow."

Chloe walked into her apartment and fell on the couch. Thankful her roommates were already in bed, she stared at the ceiling. Seeing her father had been the most emotionally exhausting thing she'd ever done. She remembered the expression on his face as she flipped through the pages of the photo album. Her whole life had been soccer for several years now. The sport completely absorbed her. And somehow it didn't seem enough.

Something was missing.

&

Trevor pushed his alarm clock off. Opening one eye, he peered at the red, digital numbers. *How can it be five thirty already?* Grabbing a pillow under his arm, he rolled over and closed his eyes again.

The phone rang.

Punching the pillow away, Trevor sat up. *Who would be calling at this hour?* He glanced at the clock that now read 9:00. *That can't be right.* He rubbed his eyes and looked again as another ring sounded. *Oh no. I'm sure it's the school wondering where I am.*

He cleared his throat and picked up the phone. "Hello." He cleared it again after his greeting came out a bit raspier than he'd hoped.

"Mr. Trevor Montgomery?"

Trevor frowned. He didn't recognize the voice, and the last thing he wanted right now was a telemarketing call. "Yes?"

"This is Walter Spence. I'm the head coach of the men's soccer team at the University of South Carolina. . . ."

Trevor dropped the phone on the bed. Surely he'd heard wrong. He'd dreamed of USC since before he'd started his own college career. The man's voice continued to stream from the receiver, and Trevor picked it up and held it to his ear.

"We have an opening for an assistant athletic trainer and would like for you to come in for an interview. How about next week?"

Trevor couldn't speak. What was happening? Was he dreaming?

"Mr. Montgomery, are you there?" Mr. Spence was asking.

"I'm here. That would be wonderful."

Trevor couldn't recall another thing they spoke about, though they talked for several minutes. Thankful for the pen and paper inside his nightstand drawer, he had been able to write down his interview day and time.

He hung up the phone. "The University of South Carolina." The words slipped from his lips. Excitement welled in his heart. He'd longed to be closer to his dad, yearned to work at the university he'd grown up around. How many USC games had his parents taken him to? Too many to count. When he was a boy, the only clothing colors he owned were garnet and black, in support of his Fighting Gamecocks. "This is my dream job." In a minute, in a second, he'd pack his things and head to his hometown.

Chloe's face filtered through his mind. He'd not been able to squelch the attraction he felt toward her. Through God's help he'd never acted on his feelings. He'd never told her how he thought of her almost every waking hour. *"It's not like we're on a date."* Her response to his offer of walking her to the door popped into his mind.

No, they weren't on a date. They never could be, and the reality of it sliced through his heart. *Maybe moving away is the best thing I could do.*

seven

Chloe sat on the bench in front of her locker in the women's locker room. The drip of a faucet in the shower area plopped to its own rhythm. She'd never before heard the place so quiet. Her ankle throbbed. She knew it was swelling again. Though she'd gritted her teeth and gripped the examining table while the doctor checked it, she had no doubt the doctor would deem her unfit to play.

"It's only been four and a half weeks since the injury, Chloe." Doc's voice penetrated her mind. *"In the best of circumstances, you shouldn't be able to play for another two weeks, but I'll take a look."*

She didn't understand why the man had acted so put out by her request. She wanted to get back on the field, help her team. It was her last year, and she'd already missed over two weeks of games. She and Trevor had been working on her ankle, and everything was going great. But now...

Why? She peered down at her foot. *Why won't you heal? For the last two weeks I've done everything Trevor told me to do.* The fact that she did nothing he'd instructed her to do the first fourteen days slipped into her mind, but she pushed the thought away. It didn't make sense that her ankle wouldn't get better. It was sprained, not even broken.

Chloe thought of the tract she'd found in her sister's purse. Curiosity at the cartoon figures made Chloe read through it. The same salvation plan she'd known since she was a child spilled from its contents. "Accepting Jesus is simple." Her

Sunday school teacher's words rang through Chloe's ears.

Sure, accepting is simple, but what if you don't believe, don't trust? Chloe folded her arms in front of her. She did believe in God. Just a glimpse of nature and she couldn't deny Someone much greater than anyone she'd ever known created it. And she saw proof of changed lives in her family. But the trust thing. It always tripped her up. Like now with her ankle. Mama had promised to pray for her, and Chloe knew she had. Trevor had said he'd pray for her, and she believed he had, as well. Chloe clenched her fist and hit the bench. *Does that mean You want it to stay hurt?*

"Sometimes God allows things to happen in our lives to draw us closer to Him." Daddy's words when he first learned he had black lung echoed in her mind. She tried to believe what her father said—after all, he never lied. And she saw his faith grow deeper and stronger as the illness worsened, but she'd never been able to understand why the pain was necessary.

What's the point in my not getting to play my senior year? Nothing good can come of it. She looked at Molly's locker a few down from hers. The girl had continued to check on Chloe, calling her on the phone, stopping by the apartment. *But I want to be the one scoring the goals.*

Maybe I have a different goal. A soft nudging touched her heart. She shook her head, unsure where the feeling came from.

The door to the coach's office opened, and Trevor stepped outside. Deep green eyes seemed to pierce her as he raked his hand through his dark hair. The mass of the man towered over her, and Chloe admitted her attraction to him. *Maybe Trevor is a goal I could have.* She shook the thought away. The last thing she needed to think about was romance. Healing, that was her focus.

"We're ready."

Chloe stood and made her way gingerly to the door. Pain shot through the side of her ankle as she walked.

"It's hurting again, isn't it?"

Chloe turned and looked into his soft, compassionate eyes. Infuriating. She didn't want his compassion. She wanted him to fix her. "No, it's not."

A slight sigh escaped his lips as he pointed toward a chair for her to sit in. Lowering herself into it, she took in the frustrated expressions of the other three men in the room—her coach, the assistant coach, and the doctor.

After clearing his throat, the doctor clasped his hands together. "I'm not going to mince words with you, Chloe. You've reinjured your ankle. You'll need another six weeks off."

Chloe jumped out of her chair. "Six weeks! There're only eight weeks left in the season."

Coach Collins stood nose to nose with her the best he could. In truth he had to look up into her eyes. He pointed at Trevor. "And this time you're going to do everything that man says."

&.

"You're going to have to rest it again." Trevor followed Chloe as she half stomped, half limped into her apartment. "It's not going to get better if you don't."

She turned toward him, her hair flipping across his face. "The stupid thing is never getting better. I might as well bundle it up and play ball."

He'd had it. The woman acted like a toddler. She was aggravating. Frustrating. Infuriating. "Do you really think you can hit a soccer ball with that ankle?" He slapped his hands on his thighs. "Maybe you can hit it, but would you be any help to your team? Who's supposed to benefit here? The team you say you love so much? Or you?"

"How dare you talk to me that way! I love my team. It's my last year, Trevor. Of course I want to play. It's my job to play." She pointed at him. "It's your job to fix me."

"I can't fix you unless you listen. We'd been working on rehabilitating it. Slowly. You've done something. Did you work out at the gym without me?" Her face turned crimson, and he knew he'd guessed right. He shut her apartment door. "And guess what, Chloe Andrews—you're back on rest and ice."

"Oh no." She shook her head then pointed to her foot. "We're going to rehabilitate this thing. Right now."

"No, Chloe." He stepped toward her and grabbed her hand. Towering over her, he peered into eyes as blue as the ocean. The storm within them radiated with fierce passion for her sport. Her strength drew him. Lowering his head ever so slightly, he realized how much he wanted to claim her lips with his own. Her head tilted backward slightly, and Trevor knew she would accept his kiss.

"What's going on in there?" Liz's voice sounded from down the hall. "What did Doc say?"

Chloe broke away from him and swallowed slowly. She'd been affected as much as he. The knowledge of it warmed his heart.

Liz walked into the living area. Renee followed and added, "Do we get our star center forward back?"

Trevor stared at Chloe. She still seemed confused by what had almost happened between them. He shook his head slowly, never taking his gaze from her. "No. She's not back."

She scowled. The moment evaporated as quickly as it had developed. "Yes, I am back."

"No. Chloe, your ankle needs rest and ice—"

"Why can't you just fix it? Rehabilitate it. Let's strengthen it."

"It has to heal first. Completely. You have to stay off your ankle. Again."

"I have to take Natalie's purse to her."

Trevor furrowed his brows. Where had that come from? "You're not driving."

Chloe rested her hand on her hip. "I can drive if I choose to drive."

She wants her independence. Trevor took a slow breath. He needed to be calm, patient with her. He'd be every bit as upset if he were in her position. "I will take you." He tried to reach for her hand, but she pulled away. "Chloe, we agreed I would take you."

"No, I'll go by myself. I'm a perfectly capable woman who gets really tired of being bossed around!"

"If you want to go to Otwell," Trevor said, trying to remain calm yet firm, "I'm going with you to make sure you stay off that ankle."

"This is your fault. I did everything you said."

He'd had it. Trying to be reasonable with Chloe was like trying to put a cast on a broken toe. It was impossible. "Everything? I doubt it." Flustered, Trevor turned toward her roommates. "She has to rest her ankle. No walking. Get her crutches—"

"No! I don't think so."

Trevor ignored her and continued to look at Liz and Renee. "If she doesn't listen to me, she won't play a single game, not even a practice, for the rest of the year."

❧

"He's infuriating, Daddy." Chloe leaned back in the chair beside his bed. "Why can't he just fix my ankle? But no. He can't do that. I have to go back on rest. . .and ice. He wouldn't even let me drive here by myself."

Her father pointed at her. "Loves you." He covered his mouth to cough then smiled beneath his closed fist.

"Oh no. I don't think so." Chloe stood and fluffed the pillows around her father. "Are you comfortable, Daddy?"

He nodded then grasped her hand in his. "Good. . .to see you."

"It's good to be here. I wish I hadn't taken so long to visit. I guess that's one good thing about Trevor. He was the one who got me here."

Daddy smiled and nodded again.

Chloe gently rubbed his forearm. "We've visited for a long time, and you look so tired." She leaned over and kissed his forehead. "I'll let you rest awhile." She grabbed her crutches from against the wall and hobbled to the bedroom door then turned to take another look at her father. His eyes had already closed, and his chest lifted and fell in labored rest. She whispered, "I'll be back in here before I leave, Daddy."

On crutches Chloe made her way into the kitchen. Her mother stood over the sink cleaning fresh carrots and celery. Sabrina scooped spoonfuls of chocolate chip cookie dough onto a baking sheet. "Where is everyone?"

Mama turned and looked at her. "Playing ball with your fellow."

Chloe huffed and leaned against the cabinet beside her mother. "He is anything but my fellow. The man is a nuisance and obviously incompetent at his job. I've been on these things forever." She lifted the bottom of one of her crutches.

"And I'm sure you've listened to all his instructions." Sabrina pointed her spoon at Chloe.

"What is it with everyone thinking I don't listen? I always listen." Chloe hobbled over to the table and plopped down.

"Ha!" Her mother dropped the vegetables in the sink and

looked at her. "This from the daughter who kicked clothes under the bed when her mother told her to clean her room and then said she'd done just as she was told. The daughter who hid her vitamins in the dog's food and promised up and down that she'd taken them."

Chloe bit her bottom lip to hold back her giggle.

"Or the sister," Sabrina began, "who didn't touch her big sister's nail polish when she'd been told to leave it alone, and yet the polish was painted all over her toes and even part of her feet."

"Come on, Sabrina." Chloe rolled her eyes. "I wasn't that bad."

"Oh yes, you were." Mama pointed a carrot at her. "And I'd be willing to bet you're still as hardheaded as ever."

"But you love me anyway." Chloe smiled at her mother and batted her eyes.

"Yes, I do." Her mother kissed the top of her head.

"If my hunch is right, so does a handsome guy out there playing basketball with my husband and siblings." Sabrina licked the tip of her spoon.

"Yeah. . .whatever." Chloe hit the air. "That man's mission in life is to exasperate me."

"Which is why he brought you all the way down here not once but twice in a week's time." Her mother started arranging celery and carrot sticks on a vegetable tray.

"That's just because it's his job to take care of the Ball State players." Chloe grabbed a carrot and popped it into her mouth.

Mama and Sabrina looked at each other and said in unison, "Yeah. . .whatever."

Chloe giggled at them. "Okay. I give. What can I do to help?"

"Now she asks." Sabrina slapped her thigh then opened the oven door and slid the cookies inside.

"All you have to do is eat." Mama stood and walked toward the door. "I'm just going to call in the troops."

Sabrina bent down and whispered in Chloe's ear, "What do you want to bet your trainer man will come running?"

"Of course he will. Everyone comes running for Mama's cooking."

Sabrina shook her head. "Nah. This time it'll be for Daddy's girl."

The notion was preposterous. She and Trevor did nothing but argue. Mama hollered that it was time to eat, and Chloe watched as the Andrews family stampeded into the house. Trevor followed, talking to her brother Gideon. He looked up, and their gazes met for a moment. He smiled and winked. *He couldn't have feelings for me. Could he?*

eight

Trevor was exhausted. His muscles ached, and the crick in his neck was a killer. Probably the drive to and from Otwell two days before and the flight to South Carolina yesterday had finally begun to take their toll on his body.

He walked into his parents' home. Though his mom had been gone for over a decade, his dad had never replaced her furniture. The paisley-printed blue-and-white curtains draping the windows and Victorian ceramic figurines adorning a corner hutch along with the overstuffed deep navy couch and loveseat made it still feel like their home. Only one item changed the room—an oversized, brown leather recliner that massaged one's back at the push of a remote control. His dad had added his "man's" chair to the otherwise feminine living room some seven years earlier.

Trevor fell into the chair, dropped his briefcase beside it then kicked off his black, tasseled dress shoes. Loosening the new deep crimson tie that had threatened to choke him for the last few hours, he leaned back and allowed the footrest to pop up.

Or maybe the exhaustion came from the interview. The last two hours had been nothing short of intense.

Four men and one woman made a horseshoe shape around a long table. He sat at the center of the horseshoe facing them. One by one the men's soccer coach, the athletics director, the women's soccer coach, the university doctor, and the man who would be his direct boss drilled him with question after question. It had been just over a half hour since he'd left, and the only question he could remember answering was his full name. The whole thing was a blur, a nervous blur. Still, the warm departure the five gave him assured him he must have done well. *Lord, I pray I did.*

The idea of being an assistant athletic trainer for the Fighting Gamecocks still sent chills of excitement through his veins. For as long as he could remember, he'd dreamed of working there.

He reminisced about many years earlier when he'd gone to a soccer game with his parents. He couldn't have been more than ten, and the mid-October weather had been much cooler than usual. Mom had bundled him into several layers of shirts and socks in addition to the long johns she'd made him wear under his pants. He'd complained about the extra load the whole way in the car as sweat beaded on his forehead. Once there, he'd been able to focus on the game, cheering his team, as many people huddled under blankets for warmth. That night his dad had surprised him with a team poster signed by the coach. Yes, he'd love to live closer to his dad again.

Sighing, he pushed the remote and let the chair massage his tense back. The mid-September weather today was anything but cool. He wiped away the perspiration that had gathered at his hairline. Closing his eyes, he leaned farther back.

"How'd your interview go?"

Opening one eye, he looked up at his dad. The years had been good to Vince Montgomery. He still carried a straight, strong stature. Only his salt-and-pepper hair and the crow's feet that fanned from his eyes revealed him to be a middle-aged man. A sprinkle of overgrown stubble dotted his jaw and chin. "I think it went well." He sat up in the chair and turned off the massager. "But I can't remember a thing they asked."

A deep chuckle filtered through his dad's lips. His eyes laughed with him. "Typical. I could never remember anything after an interview."

"They said they'd contact me. I hope it won't be too long."

"I'd say it will be fairly soon. Their guy had to quit midseason due to some kind of family circumstance."

"Yeah, but I wouldn't quit Ball State midseason. It's not fair to them."

"That's integrity talking, and I'm glad to hear it." His dad patted Trevor's shoulder. "If you're up to it, I'd like to treat you to lunch."

"Food. I'm always up for food." Trevor stood and walked toward his old bedroom. "Just let me get out of these clothes."

"I thought we'd go by and put some flowers on your mom's grave, as well."

"Okay." Trevor cringed. He hated visiting his mom's grave. He didn't understand it, either. She wasn't there. She was in heaven with Jesus. He grabbed a T-shirt and jean shorts from his suitcase. But it made Dad feel better. *I guess it's Dad's way of still being able to take care of her in some small way.* He slipped on a pair of comfortable sandals. "I'm ready."

Trevor followed his dad to his new, oversized four-by-four truck. They drove to a nearby steak house, one of his dad's favorite places to eat. Trevor loved their fried onion appetizer and prime rib dinner, as well. Once seated, he watched his dad push the menu to the side. "No need to look. I get the same thing every time."

Trevor pushed his away. "I know what I want, too."

The waitress, a woman Trevor guessed to be in her mid-forties, approached their table. She grabbed a pen from behind her ear and winked at his dad. "You want the same as always."

He nodded. "Yep."

She turned to Trevor. "And who's this nice-looking young man?" She rested her hand for a moment on his dad's shoulder. "Why, Vince, this must be your son. He looks just like you." She looked at his dad and smacked her chewing gum. "He's quite the looker."

His dad guffawed. "I'd say he's quite a bit better looking than I am." He nudged her arm. "You'd think the boy could find himself a date or two. You know I'm not getting any younger, and I'd like to see a few grandchildren before I die."

The woman swatted the air. "You're fit as a fiddle, Vince Montgomery. You let that boy be. He'll find him a wife when he's ready."

Trevor gazed at the woman's left hand—no wedding band. Their banter could be defined as nothing less than flirting. Given the amount of time his father obviously spent at the restaurant, Trevor wondered if the two might be interested in each other. Trevor swallowed and plastered a smile on his face. The idea felt weird, yet there was no reason his dad shouldn't consider dating again. The man was still young. Mom would want him to be happy and share his life with someone. The more he thought about it, the better the idea sounded.

He took in the woman's light blond hair, cut in a short, trendy style. Her pale blue eyes glimmered with a deep-down happiness. She seemed to be in good shape like his dad. She had to be since she was a waitress and spent hours on her feet every day.

The two continued to banter even after Trevor gave her his order. Throughout lunch he considered the idea. He watched his dad and the waitress talk every chance they had. What reason would his dad have for not pursuing a relationship?

More than twelve years was a long time. Surely he wanted to have some companionship.

The thought brought a picture of Chloe to his mind. Though she aggravated him to his very core almost every time he saw her, he felt more drawn to her each moment. Her zeal and zest magnetized him. Her passion was contagious. And her beauty, well, it was uncontested. In sweats, early in the morning, or made up for an afternoon out with friends, the woman astounded him.

But she's not for me. The fact that every time we see each other we get into some type of argument. The fact that she doesn't listen to a word I say, even in the area of my expertise. The fact that she's afraid to get close to people. Though he knew the visit with her parents the week before had induced a subtle change in her demeanor, she was still off-limits.

She doesn't know You, Lord.

Shaking the thought away, he determined to focus on this time with his father. He only had today before he'd have to head back to Muncie, and he didn't want to spend it pining for a girl he'd never date.

With their meal finished, his dad paid for their lunch, and they headed to the grocery store to pick up some flowers to put in the urn in front of his mother's grave. Since Trevor hadn't been to the cemetery for quite some time, his dad wanted him to pick the flowers. With Labor Day having just passed, he selected several shades of red, blue, and white.

"She'd like these." His father took them to the cashier and started to pay.

Trevor covered his father's hand with his own. "You bought lunch, Dad. At least let me buy the flowers."

His dad nodded and put his wallet back in his pocket. In silence they left the store and headed to the cemetery. His dad drove slowly along the winding road that ran past plot after plot, tombstone after tombstone. Trevor felt sick. He wasn't sure if it was the motion of the truck or the fact that they drew closer to his mother's grave.

He wanted to remember her happy. He wanted to remember her fixing dinner at the stove, bending over the washing machine to pull out wet clothes, kneeling in front of her flower garden in the yard. He hated seeing the tombstone. Glancing at his dad, he fought his frustration. Dad loved visiting it.

His father stopped the truck beside her grave. He got out, walked over to it, and traced her name with his fingertips. Gripping the flowers in his hands, Trevor slowly opened the truck's door and stepped outside. He moved to the tombstone, lifted the wilting flowers from the urn, and replaced them with his own arrangement. Fingering the flowers apart, Trevor's gaze roamed the chiseled words. "Loving wife and mother. A blessed child of her Creator."

Trevor stood to his full height and glanced at his father. He appeared to be studying Trevor's arrangement to see if it met with his approval. Shoving his hands in his pockets, Trevor shifted his weight from one foot to the other. "Does it make you feel sad to come here?"

His dad's face lit with a smile. "Oh no. I love to visit." Trevor nodded, and a shadow fell across his father's face. "Does it make you feel sad?"

Trevor shrugged. "A little."

"We can go back to the house, son. I would never want to make you feel uncomfortable. I just assumed you felt the same peace—"

"No, Dad." Trevor lifted his hand to stop him. "I want to do this with you. It's just that I like to remember her doing. . .

doing normal things, like laundry and dishes, when she was healthy."

A contented smile settled on his father's face. "Ah, me, too, son. But until I see your sweet mother in heaven, this is the only way I know of to visit her. Well, sort of visit her. I know she's not here. But this is the last place I got to see her, or her casket anyway, so. . .I guess I don't know exactly how to explain it."

Trevor watched as his father's eyes misted over. The love between his parents had been strong, true and united by their heavenly Father. It was the kind of relationship Trevor wanted. Needed.

Several minutes passed before the two stepped back into the truck. In silence his father wound around the road that led out of the cemetery. Once back on the main road, Trevor sneaked a peek at his dad. Contentment, not sorrow, etched lines into his father's face, and Trevor wondered again why he had never dated. Maybe he could never let his mother go. "You've never stopped loving her?"

His dad smiled. "Oh no. I never will."

"Is that why you don't date?"

"No. I would date."

The admission surprised Trevor, and he knew his mouth gaped open in astonishment.

His dad chuckled. "I see you're surprised."

"To say the least."

"I think your mom would be all right with me dating. I would want her to if I had passed away years ago."

"Then why don't you?"

"God hasn't shown me the right person yet."

"What about the waitress at the restaurant?"

"Betty? Oh no. We're just friends. She still struggles from

a twenty-year abusive marriage. Her husband just died a few years back from liver cancer."

"But—"

"Son, I'm not looking. But if God sticks the right woman in my life, the one He's chosen, then I won't argue with Him. God knows what I need."

His father's last sentence struck Trevor's heart. *God knows what I need, too. I don't have to worry about Chloe. I'll stay close to Him, and He'll guide my heart.*

⁓

Chloe drank in the cathedral ceilings and wide-open feel of the sanctuary. The walls were chocolate colored and trimmed with creamy white. Individual hunter green cushioned chairs sat on a lushly carpeted floor. Drums, guitars, a baby grand piano, and multiple microphones stood on an elevated stage. MAY WE KNOW YOU MORE was written in dark bold letters on a banner that hung behind the stage. "I've never seen anything like this."

Matt leaned toward her. "It's pretty cool, huh?"

"My home church is much smaller, more traditional looking. A podium. A baptistry. Piano. Pews."

"Wait 'til they start the music. You'll flip."

Chloe settled into a chair beside Matt. A kind-looking man passed by them and handed her a bulletin. She skimmed the contents and was stunned to see the multiple songs they planned to sing. They'd never get out of here. *Oh well. It's just one Sunday.* She leaned back in the chair and gazed at the people around her. "Didn't you say Trevor goes to this church?"

"Yeah, but I don't see him. He'll be sorely disappointed he missed you."

"What's that supposed to mean?"

"You figure it out."

The music started before Chloe could say anything else. The tempo was upbeat, and the drummer, guitarists, and pianist were all dressed in comfortable clothes. Glancing down at her long black skirt and button-down red jacket, she suddenly felt overdressed. She watched the lead singers, four of them. They seemed transformed by the music. They lifted their hands, and though their eyes were closed, their faces shone with awe and reverence for the One they worshipped.

Others around her started to stand, and Chloe was unsure what to do. Soon Matt was on his feet. He clapped with those around them. Chloe stood and rested her weight on her good foot. She scanned the audience, watching the faces. Several people had raised their hands and seemed to sing as loud as they could. Song after song played, the tempo flowing then ebbing on perfect cue. Something stirred in her heart. These people praised in genuineness. Chloe could feel it.

The music slowed, and Chloe broke away from watching the people. She gazed at one of the large screens behind the band. The words to the song rolled across the screen. Words of love and praise, honor and commitment. Words of longing and yearning. From God. For us.

For me?

The words pricked her spirit. She wanted to draw near to God. Wanted to know Him. Wanted to trust Him. But she was afraid. So afraid. What if He let her down? What if He allowed more sadness in her life?

The band slowed the music as a man walked onto the stage. He began to pray. By the time he'd finished, the music had faded away. The preacher laid his Bible on the adjustable metal podium. He carried it toward the center of the stage, set it down then opened his Bible. Looking at the crowd, he smiled. "Our Lord Jesus tells us in the book of John, 'I have told you these things, so that in me you may have peace. In this world you will have trouble. But take heart! I have overcome the world.'"

Chloe gripped the strap of her purse. *Oh boy. Here we go.*

nine

Two weeks had passed since Trevor had gone to his interview at USC, and he'd heard nothing. Not a word. Frustrated more than he would have imagined, he stepped out of his car and slammed the door. Walking into the Cardinals' stadium, he spied Chloe sitting on the bench. She watched the team warm up for the game. It was obvious she scrutinized each move they made as she shifted back and forth in her seat with each kick of the ball.

It pained him to look at her. She'd been able to start working her ankle again the week before, and his attraction had grown more intense the last few visits. But seeing her walk into his church a few days ago had nearly caused his heart to burst with excitement. Learning she'd attended with Matt the week he was in South Carolina had sent his mind into a gyro of emotions. Jealousy that she'd gone with another man and excitement that she'd opened her heart to attending church.

He zipped up his Ball State jacket. *Dear Lord, You're going to have to save her soul or move me away from her.* Taking a long breath, he made his way to the bench. "Hey, Chloe."

"Trevor." She looked up at him. Her face broke into the sweetest smile he'd ever seen. Her light blue eyes flickered with delight. Whether for the game or to see him, he wasn't sure. "Have a seat." She patted the bench right beside her.

"Sure." Trevor sat next to her. She whipped her head around as she watched one of her teammates dribble toward another

79

player. A whiff of strawberries floated toward him. Shaking his head, he glanced down at her bandaged foot. "How's your ankle today?"

"Pretty good." Chloe turned and peered into his eyes. Her gloss-tinted lips bowed up, causing a small dimple in her left cheek. Trevor noticed that the dimple only appeared when she offered a slight smile. "No more swelling."

Trevor raised his eyebrows. "You're listening to your trainer?"

"I am."

"Well, that's a change."

"I know. A lot of things are changing about me. It seems I have more unanswered questions, and yet the more I voice them, the more content I feel."

"So you're getting your answers?"

Her brows furrowed. "That's the funny thing. Not really. But I *feel* the answers are coming. Does that make sense?"

"Sure." *No. Not really. As time passes, I'm feeling more confused. About Chloe. About my dream job. About everything.*

Chloe looked at him. "After this past week's sermon, I've been reading Genesis."

He nodded and watched one of the girls dribble the ball to warm up. "Really?"

"Yeah. I remember studying the story about Abraham offering up Isaac when I was a small girl in our Sunday school class."

"He didn't actually sacrifice him."

"I know. God provided a ram. But Abraham was willing to. He was willing to give up his most precious possession." Chloe grabbed a bubble gum wrapper from her pocket and stuck the gum she'd been chewing inside it. "When I was a girl, I hadn't realized how precious Isaac was to Abraham. Isaac was the promised child."

Trevor nodded. "Which is why Abraham could trust God either to let the boy live or to bring him back to life."

"Yeah, but would you trust God that much? I mean, think about it. Could you listen to Him tell you to kill the thing you love most and then go out and be willing to do it? For real?"

The things he loved most flooded his mind. His dad. His dream job in South Carolina. He gazed at Chloe. The sincerity filling her face tugged at his heart. Sacrificing her would be unimaginable. "I don't know. It would be hard."

"For me it would be like having to give up soccer." Her voice came out just above a whisper.

"How do you feel about that?"

"I haven't decided."

Trevor stared at Chloe as she watched her teammates continue to warm up. Gazing at the scoreboard, he saw it would be a matter of minutes before the team members made their way over to the bench to begin the game. The urge, pure and honest, to wrap his arm around her nearly overwhelmed him. Reaching around her, he squeezed her shoulder. "I'm still praying for you, Chloe."

She turned and threw both arms around him. "Thanks, Trevor." Peering down into her mist-covered eyes, he knew she meant it.

≈

Chloe slipped into the passenger's seat of Trevor's car. Her roommates had decided to hit Pizza King for a late-night snack, but Chloe wanted to go home. Though he hadn't acted overly excited about it, she was thankful Trevor had been willing to take her. She buckled her seat belt. Trevor had spoken hardly two words to her after the game started, and she couldn't help but wonder why. If nothing else, they usually found something to argue about.

Her cell phone rang from inside her gym bag. She unzipped the side and felt her way through socks, bandages, and whatever else she'd thrown in there. Finally retrieving the phone, she flipped it open and hit the TALK button. Her mother's tears sounded before her words spilled out. Chloe listened in horrified silence. Finally, she was able to force her lips to move. "I'll be there as soon as I can." She clicked her phone shut and stared at it.

"What is it?" Trevor's voice shook with an evident knowing.

She looked over at him. He knew. Of course he knew. They'd learned so much about each other in such a brief time. But this was something she didn't want him to know intuitively. She didn't want it to be true. She wanted to open her phone, call her mama back, and beg her to take back what she'd said.

That wouldn't happen.

"My daddy." Her bottom lip quivered as tears began to spill down her cheeks. "He's gone."

"Oh, Chloe." Trevor swerved into an open parking lot and turned off the car. He leaned across the seat and wrapped his arms around her. Needing his comfort, Chloe buried her face in his shoulder. His fingers stroked her hair, reminding her of how her mother cared for her when something made her cry. "I'll take you down there tonight."

Lifting her head from his shoulder, she wiped the tears from her eyes. "You will?"

"Of course. You call your mom back. I'll drop you off at your apartment. You pack while I run back to mine and grab a few things."

"You'll take me?"

"Yes."

Chloe sat up in her seat and wiped her eyes again with the

back of her hand. "Oh, thank you."

Trevor started the car again, and memories of her family squishing into their midsize station wagon flooded her mind. He pulled into the driveway, and she remembered her daddy and mama dropping her off at this apartment four years ago. New tears poured forth, and Chloe shook her head. "I can't do it. I can't go in there by myself. Everything is reminding me of Daddy. Please go with me."

"Okay."

Trevor's gaze held such tenderness as Chloe dug through her purse for her keys. She couldn't find them. Shaking the bag, they jingled. She could hear them, but she couldn't find them.

"May I?" Trevor pointed to her purse, and Chloe handed it to him. In one sweep he pulled out her keys.

Never before had she felt so incapable, so fragile. It was as if her whole body was shutting down one part at a time. She opened the car door, and a memory of her father holding her hand as they walked to the ice cream shop after a good dentist visit danced through her mind. The remembrances wouldn't stop. They assaulted her no matter where she looked, even with her eyes shut. They were immobilizing, making her feel vulnerable.

Trevor guided her into the apartment. She sat on the bed, clutching her pillow while her trainer rummaged through her things to pack. What was happening to her? She couldn't function. *God, I needed Daddy.* Her heart filled with emotion—love for her daddy, sadness that he would go, anger that God would take him.

He was the best daddy, the best husband to her mama, the best man in the whole world. She wanted to see him again. Wanted to sit in the chair beside his bed and hold his hand. Wanted to look at her album with him. More than that, she wanted to hear his sweet baritone voice fill the porch as he picked his favorite hymns on the guitar.

Somehow she ended up back in Trevor's car. The trunk slammed, and she jumped. Trevor slid into the driver's seat beside her, mumbling something about stopping by his apartment for clothes. As she gazed out the window, memories continued to spiral through her mind.

"In this world you will have trouble." The preacher's words from two weeks ago slipped into her psyche. *"But take heart! I have overcome the world."*

"But, God," Chloe mumbled as her tears began to burn her face, "how can You overcome this pain?"

ɞ

Trevor stared at his reflection in the bathroom mirror at the home of Chloe's sister. Today was the funeral. Tomorrow he'd be back at work. With her father's passing on Friday evening, Trevor only had to take one day off work in order to stay with Chloe. Though he'd offered to get a room at a hotel, the family would hear nothing of it. But since her mother's house was packed with immediate and extended family, Trevor had stayed with Kylie and her husband.

He adjusted the knot of his mint green and navy tie. "You can do this." He buttoned his navy suit jacket. The last funeral he'd attended had been his mother's. He'd promised himself then not to go to another.

Offering to take Chloe to her family had cost him. While she slept fitfully in the car, he realized he'd be forced to attend another funeral. Unsure how he would respond and unwilling to break down in front of a family he hardly knew, Trevor had fought sickness the entire stay. He'd never felt so queasy. He was afraid wounds that had not fully healed would open and fester, so he'd spent much of his time during calling hours in the lobby of the funeral home.

He flattened the comforter on the bed one last time then grabbed his car keys from the nightstand. With extra family in for the funeral, Trevor had to stop by the Andrews house and pick up Chloe and possibly a few children.

After pulling into the driveway, Chloe stepped outside and shut the door before he had a chance to get out of his car. She slid in the passenger's side. "Hey." Her voice sounded soft and tired.

"Is anyone else riding with us?"

"No."

"Okay."

Trevor focused on his driving as he headed to the funeral home. The loss of his mother pricked his heart, and he felt true empathy for Chloe and her family. Even after all these years, he still missed her. He guessed he always would.

He stopped the car and reached for the door handle. Chloe grabbed his hand, and he turned toward her. "Trevor." The pitch of her voice rose, and she squeezed his hand tighter. The storm in her eyes brewed as tears pooled within them. "I appreciate this so much."

"It's okay."

"No." She shook her head. "You've been there for me at every step from my ankle to my daddy." With her free hand she took a tissue from her lap and wiped her nose. "Most people wouldn't do that."

It's because I love you, his heart screamed within him, and he knew it was true. Chloe Andrews was the only person on the planet who could ignite him as she did.

Her voice cracked. "Will you stay with me today?"

And every day for the rest of our lives. Trevor cleared his throat. "Of course I will."

Chloe watched as they lowered her father's casket into the earth. One of her nieces picked the guitar and sang his favorite hymn, "Amazing Grace." A hush fell over the family as the chains were lifted away and only the casket remained deep inside the ground. A sniffle sounded—then another.

A strong hand grasped hers, and she peered into Trevor's eyes. He enveloped her in his arms, and she savored his embrace. She needed his support, his warmth.

She thought of her father's face as he lay lifeless in the ornate mahogany box. Peace had filled his features. It radiated from his expression. Even in death. He was with Jesus. She had no doubt in her mind.

More than anything she wanted to be able to see him again. She knew Jesus was her only way to do it.

ten

Ten days had passed since Chloe's father died. The grieving process had been a strange one. The first few days she felt numb, almost sick from the numbness. Only pain and sadness could ebb their way into her heart at intermittent times. Those were the days she contacted her professors about the classes she'd missed. Then she'd spent a long weekend with her family. They'd sifted through her father's personal belongings, finding old love letters from Mama and notes and handmade gifts from each of the children, things they'd never known he'd kept.

The last night of her visit, Natalie's husband had taken Daddy's guitar to the porch and picked some of the songs her father had always played. Peace she'd never felt flooded her soul; then longing immediately followed. The feeling kept her perplexed the whole evening and into the next week. How could she feel peace and longing at the same time? When she thought of Daddy, peace. When she thought of moments with him, longing.

She bent down and adjusted the slim brace that enfolded her ankle. Healing was coming to a close. Finally, under Trevor's scrutiny, she was able to work out with her team. Opening the gym door, she inhaled the mixture of sweat, body odor, and rubber. Though most found the smell offensive, Chloe relished it, knowing it meant she was nearing her goal of getting back on the soccer field. Now she had newfound purpose in making it back in the game. She longed to score just one more goal in honor of her father.

Opening her locker, she placed her gym bag inside. She lifted her hands over her head and stretched as far as she could before bending over and touching her hands to the ground. She skimmed the facility, looking for Trevor. With only four weeks left in the season, she didn't want to do anything that would jeopardize her chance of playing.

She saw him at a weight bench spotting one of their freshmen players. *Brandy.* Chloe cringed. The gorgeous redhead was nothing but a flirt. More than one of her teammates had had words with the girl over her flirtatious actions with their boyfriends. Chloe had even caught her batting her eyes at Coach Collins, which was wrong for several reasons. The man was married, and he was twice their age. To his credit he never responded to Brandy, but her actions sickened Chloe just the same.

She watched as Brandy struggled to lift the bar, and Trevor's lips and body language showed him encouraging her to do so. Her face scrunched, and her arms shook as she finally hefted the bar onto its rest. Brandy popped up from the bench and clapped her hands in excited animation. Trevor smiled and nodded his head. He lifted his hand to give her a high five when suddenly Brandy wrapped her arms around him and landed a big kiss on his cheek.

A knot formed in Chloe's throat, and her heart sank. She watched in horror as the freshman nestled her face against Trevor's chest. Trevor patted her back twice then tried to move away, but Brandy held tight. Anger quickly replaced the nauseous feeling that had overcome her. She stomped over to them and placed both hands on her hips. "Trevor!"

Brandy released her grip, turned to face Chloe then crossed her arms in front of her. "Hi, Chloe. What's up?" She cocked her head to one side. "Trevor was spotting my bench press. Is that a problem?" Brandy's words were laced with a challenge.

Chloe felt her face grow warm. She had no claim to Trevor. As one of the assistant athletic trainers for the university, he helped several players on Ball State's teams. They weren't dating, merely working together to get her ankle healed.

Still, they'd spent so much time together over the last few weeks. Trevor had been a pillar of strength to her when she needed him most. She'd grown close to him—in a sisterly way. At least she had thought so.

Seeing him with Brandy's arms around his neck had instilled a new feeling within her. She hadn't seen the green monster in a long while, not since high school, but she had to admit she recognized it now. Jealousy, pure and full, had swept through her and taken over her senses.

She stepped back. Trevor was free to like whom he wanted. She didn't want him, or did she? The thought sent a whirl of emotions spinning through her, one on top of the other. Her focus had been her foot then her daddy. She wasn't ready to think about this. Whatever *this* was. "I. . ." Her voice came out soft and shaky. She cleared her throat. "I just needed to know where I should work out first."

Trevor stepped away from Brandy. "Why don't you start with some leg lifts?" His voice was soothing as he placed his hand at the small of her back and led her to an open bench. He adjusted the weight to the amount she needed. She sat and positioned her feet behind the padding, and Trevor kneeled beside her. "Did that bother you?" His voice came out in little more than a whisper.

"Did what bother me?" Chloe tried to sound nonchalant, but the shaking in her voice no doubt gave her away.

"Brandy hugging me."

"Why would that bother me? You're my trainer. I'm your trainee. It's not like we're dating or anything."

"That's all I am? Your trainer?" Trevor's voice didn't hold bitterness or anger. Instead, it begged the question to be answered.

Chloe stared into his eyes. He was more than the university's assistant athletic trainer, more than a friend. When had her feelings changed? She looked away and focused on her legs, moving the weight up and down. She couldn't tell him the truth. Not now. Not when she hadn't even had a chance to think about what she was feeling. "I don't know."

He stood, and she felt him watching her as she continued her repetitions. Trying to forget the whole conversation, she focused on her legs. They burned under the exercise, a good burn, the kind that let her know they were strengthening once again.

"I was wondering." Trevor leaned next to her once again. A rush of heat filled her neck and cheeks, and she knew they flamed red. "I have two tickets to the Colts game tomorrow."

"The Colts?" She turned and looked at him. She loved football. The Colts were her favorite team. Her family used to watch them every time they came on television. Once when she was a small girl and the coal mines were doing well, Daddy'd had the money to take the whole family to a game. She'd never forget that day.

A slow smile formed on his lips. "You wanna go?"

"Well. . ." Chloe pressed her lips together.

"As friends."

A chuckle welled deep within her. "Definitely." *The only problem is, I think I feel more toward you than just friendship.*

❧

What am I doing, Lord? Trevor shifted his weight from one

foot to the other as he waited in the concession line behind the never-ending stream of Colts fans. It was obvious something had changed between him and Chloe since the Brandy escapade at the gym. Today she'd blushed when she opened the apartment door to greet him.

Chloe only blushed when she got caught doing something she wasn't supposed to do. Maybe falling for him was something she wasn't supposed to do.

He shoved his hands in his jeans pockets as the line moved forward half a step. He'd given in to his attraction to Chloe long ago, but he still sought God's help with his love for her. She was out of reach, unattainable, not a possibility, until he knew she'd accepted Jesus into her heart.

Though she'd softened since her father's death, she hadn't told him of any commitment to the Lord.

And what about his dream job? It had been a whole month since he'd had the interview, and Trevor still hadn't heard from them. Not a letter or even a phone call. He'd pretty much given up hope on the job. *But surely they'd call me and at least tell me they'd decided on someone else.*

He moved forward again. Finally, it was his turn to order. "I'll take two souvenir drinks and two hot dogs. One with mustard and relish. The other with mustard and ketchup."

"You got it." The woman smiled and rang up his total. He handed her the money, and another woman gave him a brown paper container holding his order.

"Thanks."

The woman nodded. "Enjoy the game."

Carefully making his way past spectators who crowded at every turn, Trevor found the correct entrance and walked down toward their seats. The weather was perfect—not a cloud in sight. The sun warmed them more than usual for an autumn day in Indiana, and yet the cool breeze kept a slight "football" nip in the air. Chloe turned, and the wind blew strands of hair into her face. She smiled and pushed them away from her mouth, and for a moment Trevor wished to be a strand kissing her sweet pink lips. Her eyes danced with delight as he made his way closer. *How could a man resist her, Lord?*

"Did you have any trouble?" She reached for her hot dog and drink from the container as he sat beside her.

"None at all."

"Good. Look what I got." She laid the hot dog in her lap, held her drink with one hand, and reached down to pick up an oversized foam fist with one finger raised in the number-one sign. She giggled and raised it over her head then yelled for the team when they took the line, preparing for the snap.

He smiled and bit into his hot dog. She hadn't seemed this happy in a long time. In fact, he'd never seen her so thrilled. Between her ankle injury and her father's illness and death, he'd mainly seen Chloe having to cope with serious and hard situations. It was good, really good, to see her enjoy herself.

Leaning back in his seat, he bit into his hot dog then took a long drink. He listened and sneaked peeks at Chloe as she cheered on the team. Soon he became enthralled with the game. The score was seven to seven with only a minute left in the third quarter. The Colts had just failed to make the forty-five-yard field goal. He watched the defensive team run onto the field. The ball was snapped. The opposing quarterback launched the football like a missile through the air. The Colts defender ran toward the wide receiver. Trevor leaned forward and punched his fist through the air. "Catch it. Come on. Catch it."

The Colts player scooped the ball into his hands and ran back toward their goal.

"Yes!" Trevor flung his arms open. His hand hit something. He turned toward Chloe and gasped. Red ketchup, yellow mustard, and brown soda covered her shirt.

She squealed and jumped up, trying to brush off the ice cubes. Her hot dog flew into the air, hitting the older man in front of them. "I'm so sorry!" she cried. She leaned over and tried to pick up the hot dog, but the man threw it to the ground and waved her away.

Trevor stood stunned as she scooped up napkins from both of their seats and tried to wipe her shirt. He snapped out of his shock then and started handing her more napkins as he moved into the aisle. She stepped out, too, and hurried toward the bathroom. Still somewhat taken aback, he followed her. "I can't believe I did that."

Chloe threw a wad of napkins into the trash and turned to face him. Ketchup and mustard dotted her nose, forehead, and chin. Streaks of the condiments had even landed in her hair. "Well. . ." Chloe shook her hands as the soda dripped off her long-sleeved shirt. "This will be memorable."

"I'm sorry. I'll—"

A giggle interrupted him, and he looked at Chloe to find her wiping a drop of mustard from her cheek. She smeared the glob on his nose then broke out into full-blown laughter. "I'm a total mess." She squeezed the bottom of her shirt, and more brown liquid dripped onto the floor. She doubled over and laughed harder.

Her laughter was contagious. Trevor joined in until his cheeks and his sides hurt. "The least I can do is buy you a new shirt."

Nodding her head, she rubbed her cheeks with both hands and giggled anew when she saw ketchup and mustard covering her palms. "I think I'll let you do that."

❧

Chloe took the long-sleeved T-shirt Trevor had bought her and made her way into the women's restroom. She gasped when she saw the mess staring at her in the mirror. Grabbing several paper towels from the dispenser, she wet them then hustled into a stall. She removed her soiled shirt and wiped off as much as she could.

Her jeans were soiled, as well, but she'd just have to wear them stains and all. She rolled her eyes. *We need to get out of here—and fast.*

After unlocking the stall, she walked to the trash bin and threw away her shirt. *I'm not talented enough at doing laundry to get those stains out. I'm glad it's not one of my best shirts.* Staring into the mirror, she grabbed more towels and wiped the mustard and ketchup from her face. She opened her purse, grabbed her brush, and combed through her hair. *Ew. This is so gross. And I've definitely smelled better.* She smiled at her reflection. *But it was funny.*

A new giggle escaped her lips. That was the best laugh she'd had in a long time.

And she'd needed it.

"Thanks, God." The words slipped from her lips before she'd had time to think about them. She frowned into the mirror. *Where did that thought come from?* She bit the inside of her lip and shrugged her shoulders. Wherever it came from, it felt right.

eleven

Sweat trickled down her temple, onto her cheek, and down her neck. Chloe fumbled through her purse for her door key. Her muscles burned, and her foot throbbed but in a good way. Trevor had given her the workout of her life at the gym.

"Howdy do, stranger lady." Renee pulled open the door, nearly scaring Chloe.

"Whew. Thanks." Chloe reached to steady her racing heart. "I must have left my keys in my room."

Renee fanned her hand in front of her nose. "How did you get home?"

"Trevor."

"He must have no sense of smell. Girlfriend, you reek."

Chloe stuck out her tongue at her friend. "Hard work is what you smell."

"You've been spending a lot of time with our trainer of late." Liz walked into the living area clad in a plush purple bathrobe with her hair rolled up in a towel. Light green goop covered her face. She held a carton of mint chocolate chip ice cream in one hand and a spoon in the other.

"Aren't you the epitome of beauty?" Chloe smiled. "Date tonight?"

"Don't you try to change the subject." Liz shook the spoon at Chloe. "What's up with you and the trainer?"

Renee walked over to Liz and crossed her arms in front of her. "Yeah."

"Guess what! Trevor said next week I'm back on the practice field."

"Really!" Renee enfolded Chloe in a bear hug. She pushed away. "You really do stink."

Liz started to hug Chloe but instead patted her arm. "I can't wait until you're back out there with us."

"I know. I'm so excited." Chloe lifted her gym bag higher onto her shoulder. "I'm hitting the tub."

Dropping her stuff in her room, she grabbed a clean set of clothes and her purse. As she made her way into the bathroom, she heard Liz's faint voice. "She still avoided my question."

Chloe smiled. She knew she had done just that.

"Oh well, we'll hit her up later," Renee's voice responded.

Maybe they'll forget. Chloe shut the bathroom door then started the water. She added a capful of soap to the stream. It had been a long time since she'd had a bubble bath, and today Trevor made sure she'd earned one. She slipped into the tub then reached over the edge for her purse. She searched it for the stats Coach Collins had given her so she could study them while she soaked. Her purse fell to the floor, and she leaned over to pick up the contents, a cascade of bubbles hitting her in the face. Giggling, she blew the suds away.

One week. I'll be back on the field in just one week. She could hardly believe it. Time couldn't have moved any slower.

Daddy won't be able to collect my news clippings. A wave of emotion washed over her. She missed him so much. She'd have to visit her family before she hit the field again.

She scooped up the paper into her hands. Pushing more bubbles away, she opened the pamphlet. It wasn't stats from Coach Collins. It was the tract that had fallen from her sister's purse. *How did this end up in there? I thought I gave everything back to her.*

Thumbing through it, the words seemed to jump out at her in a way they hadn't before. She turned the page and looked at the picture that depicted God's love. "John 3:16. . ." Chloe gazed at the tile on the wall and recited from memory. "For God so loved the world that he gave his only Son that whoever believes in Him won't perish but have eternal life." She looked down at the pamphlet and smirked as she read the verse. "Well, I was close."

The meaning of the verse began to sink into her heart as she turned the page and read aloud, "For all have sinned and fall short of the glory of God." She thought of the time she'd wasted, not going to see her daddy because she couldn't bear to see him ill. He'd missed her, and she could never get that time back.

She moved to the next page. "But God demonstrates his own love for us in this: While we were still sinners, Christ died for us."

She closed the tract. Christ died for her. She'd known it since she was a small girl. He died for her. A sinner. All she had to do to receive Him was trust Him. Why was trust so hard?

The bubbles had subsided, and she gazed down at her foot in the water. No trace of injury showed on her ankle, yet she'd missed almost the entire season. *If it hadn't happened, Trevor never would have taken me to see my family. I wouldn't have seen Daddy before he died.* The realization of it weighed on her. She'd played many a soccer game. She may not play competitively after this year, but she planned to coach as long as breath remained in her body.

She'd never get time with her daddy again.

The injury caused circumstances to happen that allowed her to see him not once, but twice, before he died.

God, You have a hand in everything, don't You? And You work it all for good.

Excitement welled inside her. For the first time she realized she could trust. God was worthy of her trust. Long before she was born, He had proven himself worthy of her trust. She wanted—no, needed—to trust Him. The immediacy of it quickened her pulse. Her heart beat faster in her chest. She wanted Him to live within her. Lifting her face to the ceiling, she closed her eyes and invited the blessed Savior into her heart.

❧

Glancing at his watch, Trevor stepped into the meeting room. He still had five minutes. Letting out a long breath, he took a seat. He'd rushed home after a good, long workout with Chloe only to find that Sam Stanley, Trevor's boss, had left a message on his machine about an impromptu meeting. In barely a half hour's time, Trevor showered, shaved, dressed, and made it back to the university.

He looked around the table, noting the athletic director, Sam, Coach Collins, and the university's head women's basketball coach. A thrill crept up his spine as he wondered if they planned to give him some kind of promotion. After all, he was the only other assistant athletic trainer here, and he'd heard Sam was considering retirement. *I haven't been on long enough. I shouldn't get my hopes up. It wouldn't make sense to give me Sam's job. Besides, what about USC?*

Ten minutes passed, and Trevor wondered why someone hadn't started the meeting. He looked at his watch then at the clock on the wall. It was definitely time to start.

"He should be here any minute," Sam whispered to the athletic director.

"He'd better be good."

"He is." Sam wrung his hands. "He was top of his class, recruited by several major schools. He's perfect."

Uneasiness filled Trevor. In his heart he could sense this meeting would not be what he'd hoped. The door opened, and a light-haired man who couldn't have been more than twenty-two walked in. He nodded to each of them. "I apologize for being late. Would you believe I got a flat tire?" He wiped at his pants. They seemed wrinkle-free and clean to Trevor.

Sam stood and patted the man on the back. "You're fine, son. No one can help a flat tire. Just ten minutes past anyway." He scanned the room. "Colleagues, meet Jackson Wilcox. He's the man I'm recommending for the additional assistant athletic trainer position. I believe he has the potential to take over for me in the next few years."

Trevor's insides churned. He watched in shock as the young man shook hands with everyone around the table. When his turn came, Trevor could barely lift his hand. The man took his seat and smiled at each of them as he took résumés from his briefcase and passed them out.

Trevor scoured the contents. The man had just graduated from college at the end of the summer. As Trevor guessed, he was barely twenty-two and had zero experience. None. Except what was required for school. His grades were good enough, but the number of fast-food jobs he'd had over the last four years was a red flag in Trevor's opinion. He didn't seem to stay anywhere longer than six weeks.

Why would Sam do this? I thought I was too young to be considered, but I have six years on the new graduate. He stared at Jackson. He was definitely good-looking, and suddenly Trevor wasn't sure he wanted Jackson to be available to work with Chloe when Trevor was helping another athlete. He shook his head. *What am I thinking? I can't even ask her out on a real date because she's not a Christian. I can't keep her from seeing other men.*

The athletic director's secretary walked into the room. Though well past middle age, the woman was fit and always looked attractive. Jackson winked at her. A baffled look covered her face while pink colored her cheeks.

How unprofessional! Trevor looked around to see if anyone else had noticed Jackson's behavior. To his dismay each person was studying the younger man's résumé.

No. Trevor did not want the man working with any of the women's teams. And especially not Chloe. Sam cleared his throat. "Trevor is a wonderful asset to our university." Trevor sat up straighter. "I'd like to let him keep doing the great job he does, and I'll train Jackson." He turned to Trevor. "I called you in because I'm afraid your load may increase while we're getting Jackson situated."

Trevor could hardly believe his ears. He would have more responsibilities *and* Jackson would get preferential training. The rest of the meeting was a blur as they discussed various job descriptions, expectations, and salary. The man would even start out making more than Trevor had when he first landed his job. Jackson was too young and inexperienced to begin at such a high salary.

The whole thing was appalling.

The meeting ended, and with a mumbled good-bye, Trevor made his way to his car. He rolled down the windows and allowed the cool air to slap his face as he drove home. He needed all the help he could get to simmer down. Reaching his apartment, he jumped out of his car and made his way inside. He yanked the number to the University of South Carolina from his refrigerator and picked up the phone. Dialing, he waited as several rings ensued.

"University of South Carolina athletic office," a friendly

female voice said over the line.

"I'd like to speak with the athletic director if he is available."

"I'm sorry, he's out of the office, but I can take a message."

Trevor raked his fingers through his hair. "Sure. This is Trevor Montgomery. I had an interview with him about an assistant athletic trainer position a little over a month ago. I wanted to check the status of the position."

"Oh, Mr. Montgomery." The woman's voice grew stronger with recognition. "Mr. Spence, the team's coach, had a death in the family, so we haven't made any job decisions."

"I'm sorry to hear about that for him. Thank you for your time."

"Mr. Montgomery." The woman's voice lowered to a whisper. "If it makes you feel better, I think they liked you a lot."

Trevor felt the smile growing on his lips. "Thank you." He hung up the phone. *Yes, it makes me feel a lot better.*

❧

Chloe noted the bounce in her step as she made her way to a local Laundromat. Lugging the overflowing hamper actually felt good for the first time ever. With her ankle injured and having to hobble around on crutches, Chloe had spent the last several weeks at the mercy of her roommates when it came to getting her clothes clean. Liz had ruined two of her shirts by throwing them in the dryer when they were supposed to air dry. And if Chloe had waited for Renee to do a load or two for her, she would still be waiting. She felt confident Renee had articles of clothing in her room that could stand up and walk around.

Resting the hamper on her hip, Chloe reached to pull open the door. "Here. I'll get that for you," a female voice said from behind.

"Thanks." Chloe watched as Molly opened the door and let Chloe go inside.

"I've never seen you here before."

Chloe hefted the hamper onto a table beside two washing units. "I used to come every Tuesday, but when I injured my ankle, I had to let my roommates do it for me."

"Today's Friday."

"I know. They didn't do laundry very often."

Molly laughed. "Are you saying there's more?"

"Oh yes."

"Do you want some help?"

Chloe shook her head. "No. I just have another smaller hamper. But thanks."

She walked outside to her car, grateful she needed only an ACE bandage to get there. The last several weeks had been quite humbling for her. She depended on her roommates for laundry, for dish washing, for grocery shopping. So many things had been difficult without the use of her foot.

And the truth was, neither of her roommates completed tasks as Chloe did. She chuckled. When she'd been a young girl, she and her siblings often feigned the ability to do things as well as Mama. Sometimes Mama would give up on them and do the work herself, but usually she was too smart for those games and just made them redo the work.

Chloe carried the last bit inside and separated the wash into whites and colors. After filling three loads, she dropped her quarters into the machines and started them. She added soap to each one then plopped into a chair across from Molly.

Her teammate was flipping through a magazine about home designs. Chloe tried not to stare at Molly. She couldn't help but wonder what the sophomore would think when she found out Chloe would be practicing with the team again.

Molly had been nice to her at Pizza King and had called several times to check up on her. Molly said they were friends, and Chloe wondered if the sophomore was a Christian also. They played the same position, though, and being human was still part of their lives. If a gal threatened her spot on the team, Chloe wouldn't be jumping for joy about it.

"So how's the foot?" Molly laid the magazine on the table and looked up at Chloe.

"It's good." Chloe nodded and tried to sound nonchalant.

"Has Montgomery told you when you can come back to practice?"

Well, if that's not a coincidence. She must have heard about it from someone. "Actually, I get to practice with the team next week."

Molly leaned forward in her seat. "Chloe, that's great. We still have three weeks left in the regular season. You should get to play."

"I hope so." Chloe searched Molly's face for signs of hypocrisy, but the younger woman truly seemed happy for Chloe. Her cell phone rang from inside her purse. Berating herself for her distrustful attitude, Chloe pulled it out and pushed the TALK button. "Hello."

"Hey." Trevor's deep voice spoke, sending flutters through Chloe's veins.

"What's up?"

"I just wanted to make sure we're still heading to your mom's house tomorrow."

"Yep."

"Okay, I'll pick you up at eight in the morning."

"I'll be ready." Chloe pushed the OFF button and dropped her phone back in her purse. She looked at Molly again.

The younger woman pulled a packet of gum from her pocket. "Want a piece?"

"Sure." Chloe took it, opened the wrapper, and popped the gum into her mouth. Guilt pricked at her heart. Molly had reached out to her a couple of times now, and Chloe hadn't been as receptive as she should have been. *Help me, Lord. I may not be playing, but I want to be a good leader. I wouldn't mind having a new friend, either.* She glanced at Molly. "I'm heading to see my family tomorrow."

"I'm really sorry about your dad."

Chloe nodded. "Thanks." She twisted the strap of her purse. Making small talk with the girl who was playing her position proved harder than she imagined, yet Chloe felt a drawing toward her that she couldn't explain. "Trevor's going with me."

Their buzzers sounded, and they walked over to the washing machines. "You two seem pretty close."

Chloe pulled her clothes from the washer and shoved them into a dryer. "I don't know what's going on between us, to be honest."

"Yeah. I know what you mean. There's a guy I've been interested in for quite a while, but I'm not sure if he's right for me."

Chloe listened as Molly shared her heart. A bond seemed to form between them as they waited for their clothes to dry and then folded them when they finished. Chloe never would have imagined becoming friends with the girl who'd been playing her position, yet she felt a kindred spirit in Molly. Once finished, Chloe loaded her car with her clean clothes. Her heart spilled over with thanksgiving at the new friendship God had given her. *God, You can do anything in my life. Help me always to be willing to let You.*

twelve

Chloe scooped up the dice and rolled them. She picked up the metal shoe and moved it eight spaces. She turned to her sister Natalie and extended her hand. "I passed Go. Give me two hundred dollars, please."

Natalie, playing the role of banker for the game, gave her four fifty-dollar bills. "You guys are going to have to go through your money and trade me five one-hundred dollar bills for one five-hundred."

Their mother, Sabrina, Amanda, Kylie, and Chloe all fished through their money and traded with the bank. Mama picked up the dice to roll. Instead, she held them in her grip and looked around the table. "How long has it been since we played Monopoly together?"

Sabrina pushed a lock of hair behind her ear. "Mama, you and Kylie and I played just last week."

Mama shook her head. "No. I mean all of us."

Chloe shrugged her shoulders. "I don't know." She peered at her sisters, all so different from her. Each one was married. Each one had or would soon have a home full of children. She glanced at Kylie—she would have a biological child and two new adopted children in a matter of months. None of them had been particularly fond of sports. They had always been like the four musketeers, and she was the kid outsider.

"Well, I've been busy having babies." Amanda lifted her fussy six-month-old daughter out of her car seat.

Mama smiled. "That's true. With seven babies, you've

almost caught up with your mom."

"My boys keep me hopping with all their football and soccer practices. Soon we'll be adding basketball." Sabrina looked at Chloe. "Mike's the starting center forward for his middle school, just like his aunt."

"Really?" Chloe felt a niggle of guilt wedge inside her heart. She spent tons of time with her university team and with the girls' team she coached, but she didn't know her own nephew played.

"Yep." Sabrina beamed. "He's their leading scorer."

"I'd love to see him play."

"They're going to be in a tournament in Indianapolis in two weeks. Maybe you could come."

"I'd love to."

Mama wiped her eyes with a tissue. "You girls can't imagine how happy it makes me to see you all at this table. I wish your daddy were here."

Silence enveloped the room. Chloe shuffled her game money. "Daddy always won."

"Always," said Amanda.

"Do you think he cheated?" Kylie furrowed her brows in a straight line. "I mean, how could the man *always* win?"

Natalie huffed. "How could you think Daddy was a cheat? The man was a saint."

Mama burst into laughter. "Don't you girls go putting your daddy on a pedestal. He was a man." She leaned forward. "And if you want my opinion, I think he had to be fudging somewhere."

"Mother!" Sabrina lifted her hand to her chest. "Daddy was not a cheat."

"Come on, Sabrina." Her mother slapped her hand on the table. "The man won every time." She fanned her money then and stretched her hand across the vast property she owned on the board. "And maybe he taught me his trick."

Chloe bit the inside of her lip, holding back her laughter. Mama was definitely winning by a long shot. She folded her arms in front of her. "So how are you winning? You were always the first to go bankrupt."

Her mother leaned forward and shook her head. "I have no idea." Giggles erupted from each of the sisters.

"Hey, quiet down in there. We can't hear the game!" yelled Dalton.

"Sorry about that," Mama hollered back. She wiped away the tears of laughter that had pooled in her eyes then touched Chloe's hand. "Something's different about you."

"I bet it's that tall, dark, handsome fellow sitting in there on the couch." Sabrina popped several mixed nuts into her mouth.

"Do tell." Kylie leaned across the table closer to Chloe.

"Yeah, you can't keep secrets from your sisters," added Amanda. "It's against the rules."

Chloe grinned. "What rules?"

Amanda shrugged. "I don't know. Sister rules."

Chloe took a drink of her soda then set the glass back on the table. "I do like him."

"I knew it." Natalie clapped her hands.

"We all knew it." Amanda scoffed at her sister. "We've been waiting for her to figure it out."

"Shh." Chloe placed her finger over her lips. "Trevor doesn't know. And Amanda's right. I didn't realize it until just the other day. But that's not what's different about me."

Chloe glanced at her mother. Tears glistened in the older woman's eyes. "Am I to believe. . . Do I dare to dream that my prayers of twenty-three years have been answered with a yes?"

A smile lifted Chloe's lips. Of course her mother knew. She could always tell when things were wrong or right with each of her children. If only Daddy could have known, too. "Yes, Mama. I've asked Jesus into my heart."

"Praise God." Mama clapped her hands as squeals erupted around the table. Her sisters stood and wrapped her in a group hug.

"Hey, we can't hear the game!" Dalton yelled.

"Put a muzzle on it, little brother." Natalie, the shortest member of the family, stomped into the living area. "We can make noise if we want to."

"Now listen here. . ."

The sound of her brother and sister fussing faded as Chloe's heart filled with love for her family. *God, I understand why I didn't fit in with my sisters. It wasn't because I was the youngest or because I loved sports and they didn't. It was because they knew You and I didn't. Thank You, Jesus. Finally, I fit in.*

❧

Trevor listened as Dalton and Natalie had an arguing match over who could be loud and when. Soon Natalie walked back to the dining area. Muffled sounds floated from the women, and he heard Chloe's mother say, "You have to tell him."

Tell who? About what? Though he was an avid NFL game watcher and he enjoyed being with Chloe's brothers and brothers-in-law, his favorite team wasn't playing, so the women's noise distracted him. *Maybe just being near Chloe distracts me.*

Chloe walked into the room. Her face was flushed. "Who's playing?"

Dalton looked at her and growled. "Don't you come in here disrupting our game, too."

"I just want to know who's playing, you big meanie."

"No, you don't. You want to bother us," Dalton shot back.

Chloe swatted the back of his head. "I do not."

Trevor shifted in his seat to watch Chloe and Dalton. "Do all siblings fight like this?"

Gideon chortled. "Most grow out of it. We don't."

Trevor laughed. Chloe sat beside him on the couch then leaned close. The light scent of her perfume beckoned him, and he sat board straight so as not to grab her and plant a huge kiss on her lips. Goose bumps covered his skin when she whispered in his ear. "Who's playing?"

He coughed and cleared his throat. "The Patriots and the Bengals."

"Would you be willing to go somewhere with me right now, or do you want to wait until after the game?" She whispered again, and Trevor caught a whiff of her cinnamon gum.

"I'll go now."

"Good." Chloe stood and walked over to the coatrack. Trevor followed her. She took her jacket and put it on. "Don't forget—" She turned abruptly, slamming face first into his chest. "Oh! I didn't realize you were so close."

"It's okay." Trevor peered down at her. Pink tinted her cheeks. He cupped her chin with his hand, longing to lower his lips to hers. He'd never been so drawn to her as he was today. Maybe going with her was the worst thing he could possibly do, but he wanted to go so much.

"Where're you going?" Dalton's voice interrupted his thoughts.

"Out," Chloe snapped at her brother.

Dalton leaned forward in his chair. "Trevor, you don't have to do what she says. These women think they can rule our lives. I've got news for them—"

"Now listen here. I am not making—"

Trevor laughed. "It's okay, Dalton. I want to go."

"We'll have dinner ready when you get back," her mother called from the other room.

"Okay." Chloe moved away from him and toward the door. "Do I need my keys?"

"Nope. We'll walk."

Trevor followed Chloe through their backyard. The wind had cooled substantially in the last few weeks. Fall had come, and Trevor relished it. He noted that most of the leaves still held their green, but some had already changed to yellow, salmon, and deep orange. The grass was plush beneath their feet from the recent rain. Soon the first frost would come and force the foliage into hibernation. "Where are we going?"

"Someplace where we can have peace and quiet. There isn't much of either at my house."

Trevor shoved his hands in his pockets. "I love coming with you to your house. You have a wonderful family."

She stopped and looked up at him. "Do you really think so?"

"Definitely."

"I'm so glad." A smile formed on her lips as she grabbed his wrist, forcing his hand from his pocket. "We're almost there."

Trevor turned his wrist until her hand fell into his. Her fingertips were cold but felt soft and perfect around his. He wondered if she would break his hold, but she didn't.

"We're here." She let go of his hand and pointed to a stream. Several large trees surrounded the water on each side of its banks. A wooden swing hung from an oversized limb of one of the trees. "I can't believe this is still here." Chloe sat on the swing and swayed slightly.

"Is this where you played as a girl?"

"One of the places."

"It's nice." Trevor shuffled his feet. Why had she brought him here? To show him a stream and a swing? Did she just want to get away from all the noise?

"I have a surprise I want to share with you." She stood and made her way closer to him. "I believe it's something you'll understand."

"Okay." Trevor studied Chloe. She stepped closer to him, and his heart raced. A glimmer shone in her eyes. Her nose and lips were brushed with color from the cool air.

Though a tall woman, she stood on tiptoes, grabbed his arm then cupped her hand around her mouth to whisper in his ear. "I've accepted Jesus into my heart." She took a step back and stared into his eyes.

Trevor gazed down at her. "You have?"

She closed her lips, her eyes glistening with tears, then nodded her head.

"Oh, Chloe." Trevor pulled her into his arms. The love he felt spilled from within him. He'd bottled it, tied it, held it back as long as he could. Releasing her only at arm's length, he caressed her cheek with the back of his hand. A lone tear streamed down her face, and he brushed it away.

Sweetness radiated from her eyes, and he could take it no more. Lowering his lips to hers, he kissed her with the strength of the emotions he'd tried so hard to hold at bay. She received his kiss, and he felt as if his body might leave the ground in flight.

He released her, and she cuddled against him. He kissed the top of her head. "You don't know how long I've waited to hear you say those words."

"Am I to think you have feelings for me?" she murmured.

"Oh yes. Since the first moment I saw you."

"Really?"

He nodded and released his hold of her. "I've prayed for you to receive Christ more often than I've prayed for anything in my life. I even begged God to take you out of my life if you wouldn't receive Him."

"I'm glad He didn't take me out of your life."

"Me, too. Nothing can keep you from me now."

thirteen

Chloe slipped on her black pants and buttoned the waist. She grabbed her silver necklace with the oversized blue gem and fastened it around her neck. Fidgeting with the collar of her deep blue, button-down silk shirt, she scanned her closet for her black heels. She found them, slipped them on, and stood in front of the full-length mirror. The shirt and necklace brought out the color of her eyes. The pants, long enough to span her legs, rested midway down her heels.

The extra height on her five-foot, eleven-inch frame usually made her uncomfortable—but not when she stood next to Trevor. He was one of the few men she'd met who still towered several inches above her. And she loved it.

Twisting, she stared at her reflection. She combed her fingers through her hair. She looked nice. Felt pretty. Not sporty, not tomboyish, but feminine and attractive. *I could get used to this.*

Grabbing her purse from the bed, she walked into the living area and glanced at the clock. Trevor would be there any minute.

"Wow. You look nice." Renee unfolded her legs and set her cereal bowl on the end table. She reached over and touched Chloe's shirt. "Soft."

"Where're you going?" Liz blew on the top of her coffee cup.

"Church."

"Again?" Liz furrowed her brows. "But you didn't get back from your family's house until like midnight last night."

113

"I know."

Liz popped a grape into her mouth. "Isn't this like the second or third time?"

"Third. You guys could go with me if you want."

"No thanks." Renee folded her legs back under her.

"Are you going by yourself?" Liz seemed interested, which encouraged Chloe.

"Trevor's coming to get me."

Liz snorted. "That's why you're going."

"No. I'd go without him." Chloe peeked out the window and saw that Trevor had pulled up. She looked back at Liz and Renee. "If you want to, we could all go together next week."

"Count me out," Renee said, grumbling.

Liz shrugged.

The doorbell rang, and Chloe walked to the door. "Okay. I'll see you guys later." *God, if You can change me, You can change anyone.*

Opening the door, she bit her bottom lip as a wave of excitement and sudden embarrassment hit her at the thought of Trevor picking her up as a date. "Hey." She fiddled with her purse strap.

"Hey." He bent down and kissed her cheek. "You look beautiful."

Contentment flooded her heart. She wished so much that Daddy could see how happy she was now, even without playing soccer. One day, in heaven, she'd tell him all about it.

❧

Trevor settled into a seat beside Chloe. Scanning the church sanctuary, he saw Matt approaching them. A wave of jealousy washed over him at the thought of Matt flirting with Chloe. He pushed the feeling aside. God had been working on Matt's heart, and Trevor needed only to encourage him.

"Hey, Matt." Trevor waved and patted the seat beside him. "Why don't you join us?"

"Sure." Matt shook Trevor's hand then pushed his way to the open seat beside Chloe.

Great. Now I have to listen to him flirting with Chloe. Lord, I won't be able to handle it.

"So did you two finally decide to make yourselves an official couple?" Matt's voice interrupted his thoughts.

"Yep." Chloe's smile lit up the room. She gingerly took Trevor's hand in hers.

"It's about time. Watching you two was giving me a headache."

"What was giving you a headache?"

Trevor turned at the female voice beside him. He peered at one of Chloe's teammates. What was her name?

"Molly." Surprise sounded in Chloe's voice.

That's her name. I haven't seen her at church before.

"I'm glad you came." Matt's voice sounded more hesitant than Trevor had ever heard it. He turned and noted that the man's face burned crimson.

"How could I resist an invitation to church? I've been looking for a church home since I transferred to Ball State." The tiny blond ran her fingers through her short hair.

Matt stood and motioned for her to sit beside him. "I'm glad you couldn't resist. Maybe I can convince you to have lunch with me afterward."

"How about just church? Maybe I could meet you at a Bible study sometime."

Matt frowned, and Trevor wondered how many times the guy had been turned down. Still, Trevor was glad the girl hadn't fallen for Matt's charms. He knew Matt could be a wonderful person, but Trevor hoped he would focus on getting to know the Lord before he found himself a girlfriend.

Molly turned to Chloe and Trevor. "I didn't think I'd make it. It's been quite a morning."

"I'm glad you're here." Chloe patted her leg.

Molly studied Chloe. "You know, you look different."

Chloe smiled. "I can't wait to tell you all about it."

Trevor's heart soared. Chloe did look different. She was the most unique person he'd ever met before she accepted Jesus; now she had the sweet, Christ-filled spirit to match. The music started, and Trevor stood with the congregation, lifting his voice in praise for God's blessings.

An off-key noise sounded from somewhere. Soon a slight squeak followed. He frowned and shook his head. Where was that noise coming from? He looked at the stage. Maybe some of the equipment or one of the microphones wasn't working right.

He heard the noise again and peeked over toward Chloe. She was lifting her hands toward the heavens. Her eyes were closed, and her mouth moved with the words of the music.

Turning away from her, Trevor closed his eyes and focused on the words. *Okay, Lord, You tell us to make a joyful noise to You. And that doesn't mean it has to be perfect.*

He sneaked another peek at Chloe. He could see the sweet expression of worship on her face, and he couldn't help but adore her openness of praise.

The music ended, and Chloe leaned close to him. "I don't usually sing in church."

He nodded. This was probably true. He'd seen her at only one other church service, and he'd noticed she didn't sing then.

"I don't sing very well. My brothers used to torture me about it, but my parents insisted we sing when we were supposed to." She looked toward the cross that hung at the front of the sanctuary. "Now I find I love singing. I feel so close to God, so much in reverence and awe of Him."

"That's all that matters." He grabbed her hand and squeezed it tight. "Our praise is always pleasing to the Lord."

She peered up at him and smiled. Her eyes shone like the sky on a clear day. "Thanks, Trevor."

No. Trevor inwardly shook his head. *Thank you for reminding me what true praise is all about.*

ॐ

Chloe stepped to the side as Trevor opened the door to the restaurant that was known for its breakfast. He placed his hand at the small of her back and guided her in. His gentle touch sent tingles through her. She'd never felt cared for as a woman. Sure, she'd thought Randy had cared for her as a man did for a woman, but they had been so young, still in high school, and she had been foolish. Now she could honestly pray that he and his wife were happy.

The waitress led them to their booth. Chloe slipped into one side and picked up the menu. Gazing at the many breakfast dishes, she had a sudden longing for one of her daddy's cheese, tomato, and green pepper omelets. As a small girl she'd scoffed at the idea of putting those nasty vegetables in her mouth. Daddy had pulled the food away. "I'll be more than happy to eat your share." He'd licked his lips and cut off a piece. Shoving the piece in his mouth, he'd rubbed his belly, declaring it the best food in the world.

His antics were too much for a small girl, and Chloe ended up taking the omelet back. She was surprised when she bit into a small piece. The spicy taste had been yummy, and she actually liked the feel of the cooked tomatoes on her tongue.

"I'd like you to meet my dad." Trevor's voice broke her reverie.

"I'd love to."

"He's flying in from South Carolina when soccer season is over."

"That'd be great."

The waitress returned and took their orders and the menus. Chloe folded her hands on top of the table and looked at Trevor. He furrowed his eyebrows and rubbed his jaw. Chloe frowned. "What's wrong?"

Trevor twisted the cloth napkin in his hand. "What are we, Chloe?"

"What do you mean?"

"I mean, I'm your trainer. I work at the university you attend."

"Is there a problem with your working for Ball State and my being a student? After all, I'm twenty-three years old. It's not as if I'm a minor or something."

"No. I don't think there's a problem with that. I just mean. . ." He picked up the fork and knife and placed them back in the napkin, folding them one way and then another. "My feelings for you are strong."

Chloe rested her hand on his. "I told Matt we're a couple." She swallowed. "I think we're definitely more than friends."

"Definitely. So what do we say?"

"We're dating?" She shrugged her shoulders, and heat suddenly warmed her cheeks. She felt more like a teenager than a grown woman. And yet the innocence and newness of their relationship felt wonderful and refreshing. "I want to be your girlfriend."

Trevor intertwined his hands with hers, lifted them to his lips, and kissed the tips of her fingers. "I think I'll like saying Chloe Andrews is my girlfriend."

fourteen

Chloe joined her teammates on the practice field. Elation filled her when Renee kicked the ball to her and Chloe felt no pain in kicking it back. The stiff bandage around her ankle was a bit aggravating but an easy compromise to be able to return to the field. She glanced at Trevor and Coach Collins on the sidelines. They were deep in conversation, and she hoped Trevor was telling him she was okay to play. *This is my chance to prove I can do it.*

She lined up with her teammates in three rows inside the penalty box. Their objective was to dribble the ball around a maze of cones. The first row of players to finish without knocking over any cones won. She got in the middle line, noting Molly stood to her right and Liz to her left. No question she'd beat Liz, but Molly—she wasn't sure.

Controlling the ball with her feet, Chloe dribbled around the first cone then the second. Molly and Liz kept pace beside her. They went around the third then the fourth. Liz knocked over a cone. Now she had only Molly to contend with. Knowing Coach Collins watched, Chloe made her way around the fifth cone. A sharp pain bolted through her ankle. She grimaced but continued. The sixth cone. Molly pushed ahead of her when they dribbled to the out-of-bounds line and back to the cones in reverse order.

Trying to pick up lost ground, Chloe dug in her heels and cut the ball sharp against each cone. She still trailed Molly by only a fraction of a step. Kick. Slice. Kick. Slice. Only one cone to pass. She kicked the ball harder than she'd intended to pass the last cone. To compensate, she extended her leg and caught the ball with her injured ankle instead of her foot. Fire whipped through and brought sudden tears to her eyes. She dribbled back to the starting line just behind Molly.

"You okay?" Molly turned to Chloe then took a long, deep breath and blew it out.

"Sure." Chloe wiped the tears from her eyes and sniffed. The wind brushed her face. She tried to chuckle. "Makes me tear up."

Molly lifted her hand for a high five. "That was pretty good footwork for a gal who hasn't practiced in weeks."

Chloe grabbed her side and squeezed the cramp. "Thanks."

Practice continued, and Chloe had never felt so exhausted. *I've been out of regular practice for nine weeks. It feels like nine years.* Sucking in a long breath, Chloe determined to keep up with the other girls. She would not quit, even if it killed her. Finally, Coach Collins blew his whistle then yelled, "That's it! Good practice, ladies."

Exhilaration kept her feet moving. She'd made it through the whole practice. She'd probably spend the evening soaking in the tub and the next morning moving at a snail's pace wishing someone would take away the misery of her muscles, but she'd stuck it out the full three hours of practice.

"Andrews, come here." Coach Collins motioned for her. Trevor stood beside him. She couldn't decide if concern or pride marked his face. She knew he didn't think she'd make it the whole practice. He'd told her to sit out if her ankle hurt. Well, of course it was going to hurt a little. She hadn't *really* worked it out in weeks.

"What's up, Coach?" Chloe took a long drink of water then plopped onto the bench. The muscles in her legs and back immediately tightened. *Oh boy, I'm in for some pain. Note to self: Take some naproxen immediately when I get home.*

"Trevor wants to check your ankle."

Chloe's heart thudded against her chest when Trevor bent down in front of her. He unlaced her shoe and slipped it off. Reaching for the top of her sock, she giggled. "I'd say it's not going to smell so hot. You want me to do that?"

Trevor grinned and whispered, "You're incapable of smelling any way but wonderful."

"Ha-ha. Very funny." Heat rushed to her cheeks, and she looked up at her coach. He was talking with Molly, and Chloe sent up a silent prayer of thanks that he hadn't heard Trevor. She cocked her head and shrugged her shoulders. "Suit yourself."

Trevor pulled off her sock and shin guard. Wrinkling his nose, he fanned the air. "I take it back."

"Hey!" Chloe punched his shoulder, and Trevor laughed. He unwrapped her brace and checked out both sides of her ankle.

"Does this hurt?" He twisted her foot slightly to the right.

"Nope." She shook her head.

"How about this?" He twisted to the left.

A shot of pain raced down her foot. "Not. . ." Everything in her wanted to tell him it didn't hurt, but she couldn't lie. "Not too bad."

A slow smile spread over Trevor's lips. "Thanks for being honest." He moved closer to her and patted her knee. "Guess what. It's going to hurt a little bit. It's stiff from not being used as much."

Relief flooded her. "So when—?"

"You can play in the next game."

Her heart pounded in her chest. "You mean it? Three days?"

He nodded and turned toward Coach Collins. "She can play in the next game."

"Wonderful." Coach shook Trevor's hand then turned to Chloe and shook hers, as well. "I'm glad you're back." He looked at Trevor. "Can I talk with you a moment?"

"Sure." Trevor stood and squeezed Chloe's shoulder then followed her coach.

Molly sat on the bench and wrapped her arms around Chloe. "I'm so happy you can play again."

"Me, too." Chloe leaned over and put her brace and sock back on. She glanced at Molly. "Are you really happy I'm healed?"

Molly frowned. "Of course I am."

Chloe sat up, searching Molly's expression. The Holy Spirit had changed Chloe. She realized how selfish she had been. If she were in Molly's shoes, she would want the injury to last the whole season. "It's just that. . ." Chloe bit the inside of her lip. "Well, we play the same position and. . ."

"You think I'd want you to stay injured, right?"

Chloe shrugged.

"Remember when I told you about having to sit out my whole senior year of high school? That was really hard for me." Molly rubbed her hands together. "If it hadn't been for my relationship with God, I wouldn't have made it."

"We haven't actually talked about it, but I thought you might be a Christian."

"Oh yes."

"I figured." Chloe picked at a piece of lint on her shirt. "I mean, you were at church on Sunday, and you've always been—well, different from other people. Like Trevor and my family."

Molly hugged Chloe again. "That's the best compliment

you could ever give me."

Chloe felt the smile growing on her face. "I'm a new Christian, too."

Molly clapped her hands. "That's wonderful. The best decision of your life."

"Yeah." She pointed to her chest. "I feel a peace I've never known before." Chloe listened as Molly shared about different things God had done in her life. Molly suggested several Bible studies Chloe could think about doing. She felt their friendship blossom even more as Molly talked, a friendship based on more than what Chloe wanted or could get out of it. A friendship based on faith.

Chloe understood why Molly was truly happy her ankle had healed. She wanted what was best for Chloe. In an instant she felt the same for Molly.

❧

Trevor walked into his apartment and dropped his keys on the table. After kicking off his shoes, he opened the refrigerator and grabbed a bottle of water and a container of leftover soup. He set the container in the microwave and turned it on. Gazing at his answering machine, he noted two messages. He pushed the button. The first message—a hang-up call—he deleted. The microwave beeped. He took out his soup and stirred it with a spoon.

"Mr. Montgomery, this is Walter Spence from the University of South Carolina," the man's voice said over the machine.

Trevor dropped the spoon into the bowl. So much had happened over the past week, he hadn't even thought about the job at USC.

"I'm sorry it took so long for me to get in touch with you. I had a death in my family. . . ."

Yes. The receptionist told me. His dream job may be a possibility. The idea seemed surreal, unattainable.

"We'd like to offer you the position. I know you've been working primarily with the women's soccer team at Ball State, but if at all possible, I need to meet with you. . ."

The rest of the message faded away. The University of South Carolina was offering him the position.

He pumped his fist in the air. "Yes!" he yelled through the apartment. No one could hear him, and he didn't care. His dream job. He had his dream job. An additional perk—he'd live near his father. *It's too good to be true.*

A beep sounded, notifying him the message had ended. He'd have to listen to the whole thing again.

Chloe's face popped into his mind. He fell into his over-sized recliner. "Chloe." What would he do about her? She had another semester of school left at Ball State, some ten and a half hours away from USC. *That's okay. We can have a long-distance relationship until she graduates. Then. . .*

Then what? Was he ready to ask her to move all the way to South Carolina with him? That sounded a lot like a marriage proposal. Were they ready for that? He leaned back in his chair and stared at the ceiling. She'd also been excited about spending more time with her family. Moving to South Carolina would put a lot of distance between her and them.

His cell phone vibrated in his pocket. Shifting in his chair, he grabbed the phone and pushed TALK. "Hello."

"Hey, Trevor," Chloe's sweet voice said.

"Hey. You had a good practice."

A sigh sounded over the phone. "Thanks, Trevor." Her voice caught, and she paused. "It's been a good day."

A good day? Yes, it had been a good day for him, as well. The job he'd wanted for years had been offered to him, but it would take him away from the woman he'd fallen in love with.

"It sure has." He continued to stare at the ceiling, wondering if or when he should tell her his "good news."

"I'd like to do something to celebrate."

"Well, let's see." He scratched the stubble on his chin. "Have you ever been to that state park in New Castle?"

"Summit Lake?"

"Yeah. That's the name of it."

"Oh yes. That was one of our vacation spots when I was growing up. It was a park, which meant free." She laughed. "I have a lot of good memories from there."

"We could go for a picnic."

"That's a great idea."

"You don't have practice tomorrow, right?"

"Nope. Coach has some family thing he has to go to or his wife is going to kill him."

"No classes, either?"

"Nope. My classes are on Mondays, Wednesdays, and Fridays."

"Let's go tomorrow then."

"Sounds good."

"It's a date."

He heard her gentle sigh over the phone. "Definitely a date."

Trevor pushed the OFF button on his phone with a growl. He wanted to spend time with Chloe. Wanted to get to know her more. To date her. To love her. To marry her. But he'd known her only a few months, and commitments took time to develop.

And his job offer. He'd wanted this job since he was a boy. For years.

He stood and walked into the kitchen. As he took a swig

of his water, his kiss with Chloe filtered through his mind. He slammed the bottle onto the counter. No doubt about it. He loved her. He'd prayed either God would move him away from her or she would accept Jesus into her heart. She'd accepted Christ, and he had the chance to move. The decision rested in his hands.

He leaned his elbows on the counter and combed his fingers through his hair. "Oh, Lord, what do You want me to do?"

fifteen

Trevor tapped the top of his steering wheel, waiting for the light to turn green. *I'm just going to take her with me. Have a long-distance relationship until she graduates in May, then ask her to move to South Carolina, too.*

He pushed on the gas when the light changed. Looking at his reflection in the rearview mirror, he nodded. *It'll work. Maybe she can get a job with the Gamecocks, as well. We could travel to see her family as often as she likes.*

Turning into her apartment parking lot, he shifted the gear into PARK. *By then we'll feel ready for marriage.* He nodded again. *Yes, it makes sense. And if our relationship doesn't work, we'll part ways, and I'll still be working at the job I've always wanted.*

He growled. Sure, his idea made sense, except that it was selfish and completely unfair to Chloe.

He looked up as Chloe opened her front door. *She must have seen me pull up.* A breathtaking smile slid across her face. She gave him a little wave then reached back inside and hefted a cooler into her arms. Trevor sucked in his breath. He had no intention of parting ways. She'd intrigued him before she'd accepted Christ. Since then the obvious change in her demeanor and spirit had only heightened his feelings for her.

He threw open the car door, bounded up the walk, and grabbed the cooler from her hands. She stood on tiptoe and kissed his cheek. "Hey, good-lookin'."

Noticing her red shirt, khaki jacket, and dark jeans, Trevor let out a whistle. "I'd say you're the good-looking one."

Her giggles warmed him as she headed for the car. Opening the driver's side door, she pushed the button to open the trunk. "I've been looking forward to this all day." She walked to the back of the car and watched as he set the cooler inside. "I hope you like what I fixed."

He shut the trunk then turned toward her. "If you fixed it, I'll like it."

A Cheshire-cat smile formed on her lips, and she cocked her head and raised one eyebrow. "You have no idea if I have any culinary abilities, Mr. Montgomery. I may send you reeling, wishing you'd never asked me"—she placed her hands on her hips and batted her eyes—"to be your girlfriend."

Her teasing worked on him like ice on a sprain, and he grabbed her in his arms and kissed the tip of her nose. A growl formed from deep inside him. "I'm not after your cooking abilities—just your kisses."

Crimson colored her cheeks as she lifted her lips to his for the briefest of kisses. He reached to pull her close, but she escaped his grasp, winked, and hopped into the passenger seat.

Pulling his keys from his pocket, he slipped into the driver's seat and started the car. Soft perfume filled his senses. "You always smell so good."

"It's Beautiful."

He laughed. "You're in a good mood and fishing for compliments? You're quite flirty, too."

Chloe wrinkled her nose and hit his arm. "Beautiful is the name of the perfume." She crossed her arms in front of her. "And if my flirting is bothering you, I can definitely stop."

Staring at her pouty expression, he caressed her cheek with

the back of his hand. "Never stop."

"I won't." She looked back into his eyes. The promise held within her gaze was that of commitment. He knew in his heart that she was meant for him, the one God had intended. There was no "if our relationship doesn't work out." This one would stand the test of time.

After turning onto the straight stretch that led to New Castle, Indiana, and their park destination, Trevor gently took Chloe's hand in his. Her fingers felt perfect within his grasp. He glanced down at her hand, noting her short fingernails. She no doubt kept them clipped because of the abuse they took from her sport of choice. He liked that they weren't manicured. To him, they proved her willingness to work hard, to give up a luxury many women enjoyed, for the love of something she held dear.

He peeked at her as she brushed strands of light brown hair away from her face. He wanted her love, yearned for it. Deep within him he sensed she was falling in love with him. Pleasure filled his heart. *She'll be willing to go with me, Lord. There'll be no problem at all.*

ta

Chloe's heart drummed faster as they neared Summit Lake Park. Her parents couldn't afford to take them on vacations to Disney World, the Grand Canyon, and other famous places, but they always managed to conjure up the means to visit one of Indiana's state parks. Summit Lake had been a family favorite.

"I have a little surprise for you." Trevor parked the car near a camping area. Picnic tables and a playground sat shaded beneath large trees adorned with red, orange, and yellow leaves.

Her eyes widened. "You do?"

He twisted his mouth in contemplation. "But you have to tell me. Do you want to eat now or later?"

She bit the inside of her lip, considering the several hours it had been since she'd eaten her cream-cheese-covered strawberry bagel. But she had nibbled bits of tuna fish salad and fresh fruit pieces as she prepared their lunch. "I can wait."

"Good." Trevor jumped out of the car, raced over to her side, and opened the door for her. Taking her hand in his, he helped her out of her seat. "Follow me."

He held tight to her hand as he made his way down a beaten trail. A cool wind breezed through her hair, kissing her cheeks and nose. The sun shone high, heating her some, but the touch of Trevor's strong hand warmed her in a comforting, belonging way that she relished to the tips of her toes.

Breathing in the fresh scent of nature, Chloe took in the trees towering around her on each side. God's arrangement of color—the shades of green and brown with splashes of autumn yellows, burnt oranges, and almost pink reds—was better than anything she'd seen a florist put together.

A tiny salamander scurried across the path in front of them. The urge to chase the little fellow into the wooded area stirred within her. She and her siblings used to collect as many as they could to scare Mama. She always pretended fear and would holler for their father to do something with his children. They would double over with laughter, the whole time knowing the little things didn't scare Mama one bit.

Shaking her head, she focused on the path ahead of them. Soon the trees cleared, and the lake appeared. She drew in her breath at the majesty of the deep blue water. Visions of paddleboating with her siblings danced through her mind. She always ended up with her twin brother, Cameron.

They paddled with all their might to catch up with their big brothers and sisters. By middle school they were finally strong enough to keep up. *Never could beat Dalton and Gideon, though.*

Trevor led her onto a dock then pointed down at a small boat. "Well, climb aboard."

"You rented a boat?"

"Yep. Called yesterday and reserved it. A friend of mine owns the rental boats. I picked up the key from him."

She clasped her hands as adrenaline rushed through her. They'd never rented a motorboat. Never been to the middle of the lake. Trevor stepped into the boat then took her hand in his. Her leg shook as she stepped gingerly into the swaying vehicle. Sitting in the seat beside Trevor, she watched as he bent down, picked up a life jacket, and handed it to her. "Thanks."

After pushing her arms through both sides, she snapped the locks in front of her and tightened them as much as she could. She pulled her hair out from beneath the jacket and released it, letting it flow over the top. Trevor unlatched the rope that attached the boat to the dock and let the boat drift out into the lake. The hum of the engine started with the twist of the key, and Trevor drove toward the center. "What do you think?"

"I think I can't believe it took me this long to accept the Lord." Chloe drank in the beauty of the lake. The deep blue beneath her. The greens and autumn splashes around her. The clear sky above cradling a smattering of cottony clouds. The smell, clean and pure, drew her, and she closed her eyes and inhaled deep breaths of God's fragrant gifts to the earth.

"It is amazing, isn't it?"

"He is amazing, Trevor." She leaned forward against the edge of the boat, watching the slight waves that formed from their boat's slow movement through the water. "How could it have taken me this long to believe in Him?"

"It doesn't matter. You believe in Him now."

"But I could have known Him years ago. Think of the people who've come into my life that I could have been a witness to."

"You know Him now." Trevor's voice took on a strong air, and he moved closer to her. "God tells us in Ecclesiastes there's a time for everything. He knows the right time, which leads me to something I wanted to tell you—"

"But my daddy died without knowing of my decision." Her mouth suddenly parched, she stood up to grab a drink from the small cooler at the back of the boat. "I was the only one—"

The boat bounced slightly in the water, and Chloe's leg hit the right side, knocking her off balance. Swinging her arms around, she tried to steady herself. She watched Trevor, almost in slow motion, reach for her.

But he was too late.

Her head and shoulders hit the water first.

ও

Trevor sat at the picnic table, waiting for Chloe to come out of the bathroom. He was thankful he had a pair of jogging pants and a sweatshirt in the car. At least she'd have something dry to wear. He arranged the paper plates Chloe had packed in the cooler. The tuna salad sandwiches looked delicious, and with it being well past time for lunch, he admitted he was glad she wanted to go ahead and continue the picnic despite her dip in the lake.

He grinned, remembering the stunned look in her eyes

when the life jacket bobbed her straight up in the water. She'd laughed and snorted so hard when he lifted her back into the boat that he nearly lost hold of her several times from trying not to laugh.

And I almost got to tell her about the job. He snapped his fingers. Leaning his elbows on the table, he lifted a quick prayer for another good opportunity to tell her about South Carolina.

"Not exactly how I planned to look for our picnic."

Trevor turned at the sound of her voice. His heart quickened its pace on seeing her. His clothes hung on her frame, which was much smaller than his. Clean of all makeup, her nose and cheeks were pink from the cool air. Her hair, full and disheveled, looked as pretty to him as when she fixed it. "Your hair's dry?"

"Automatic hand dryer." She made a turning gesture with her hand. "I just turned the nozzle around." She lifted her hair on one side. " 'Course the only comb I had was my fingers. So what you see is what you get."

Trevor stood and grabbed both of her hands in his. "I think you look good." He wiggled his eyebrows. "Real good."

She patted her stomach. "Well, I'm *real* hungry. I'm glad you have the food ready."

They walked to the table and fixed their plates. Trevor asked a blessing on their food then took a bite of his sandwich. Within moments they'd finished the food, and he threw away their trash while Chloe packed what was left in the cooler. He carried the cooler back to the car and put it in the trunk. Chloe peered up at him. "Was there something you were going to tell me in the boat before I decided to take a little dip?"

My chance. Thanks, Lord. "Yeah. . ."

"Oh." Chloe pointed to one of the swings in the playground area. "Can we go sit on the swings while you tell me?"

"Sure."

Chloe grabbed his hand and practically skipped to her destination. Flopping onto the flat rubber-covered board, she gripped the chains extending from the top board with both hands. As she began to swing lightly, tears gathered in her eyes.

"Are you okay?" Trevor reached over and wiped her cheek with his thumb.

"I'm sorry, Trevor. So many memories have invaded my thoughts today. They've been wonderful, just. . . overwhelming."

"Do you want to share what you're thinking right now?"

She pushed her swing higher as a slight smile formed above her quivering chin. "You know I'm the youngest out of the eight children. There're five girls, but the first four were close together, then two boys, then Cameron and me. By the time I was old enough to play, my sisters all cared more about boys and makeup than they did about spending time with a kid sister. Which meant I had to play with—"

"The boys."

"Yeah."

Trevor watched as she wrapped her arm around the chain and brushed more tears from her cheeks. He wanted to stop her, to enfold her in his arms and let her cry, but he could feel she needed to share this with him.

"One year," she continued, "we came here, and my sisters settled into four swings. I ran up beside them and jumped on a fifth one. They went higher and higher until I thought they would flip over the top. I tried to do it with them. I pushed my legs forward then backward, forward then backward, but I just couldn't get my swing to move."

"How old were you?"

"I don't know, maybe five. Cameron could do it by himself, but for some reason I just couldn't get the hang of swinging."

Chloe slowed her swing, and Trevor followed beside her. "The girls started teasing me. I wanted to cry, but instead I just yelled at them, calling them every mean name I could think of. The girls hollered for Daddy. He came running toward us. He listened while the girls told him the things I'd said."

Chloe stopped her swing and twisted back and forth. "Daddy sat there and looked at me for several minutes. I clutched the chains as tight as I could, expecting him to let me have it for the things I'd said. Finally, he smiled and walked behind me. Pushing from behind, he said, 'Girls, I think Chloe just wants to play with you.'"

"And he was right." Chloe stood and stepped away from the swing. Trevor watched her inhale slowly. "I never fit in with the girls." She looked at Trevor. "Until the last visit."

She smiled and walked toward him. "I guess it's because I'm older." She shook her head. "No. It's because of the Lord. Or maybe it's both, but you know my sisters and I bonded. Truly bonded. I can't wait to get to know them better. When I graduate next spring, I'll be able to move close to them all again and make up for lost time. Did you know Kylie even called me the other day just to tell me about her baby checkup? It was wonderful, Trevor. Truly wonderful."

Trevor stood and wrapped his arm around her. "I'm happy for you, Chloe." Uncertainty warred within him as they walked together toward his car. He couldn't ask her to leave her family. If she said yes, she'd be miserable. If she said no, he'd be crushed. *Lord, I thought the plan made sense. I thought it was all worked out.*

Chloe lifted her hands to her lips. "Trevor, you were going to tell me something?"

"Not a big deal." He bent down and kissed her lips gently. *It was just my dream that has come to fruition, but if I take it, I lose you.*

sixteen

Chloe tightened the brace around her foot. After slipping on her shin guards and socks, she put on her cleats and laced them tight. She shimmied her Sweet Spots over the laces to ensure they didn't have the chance to come untied and trip her again. Standing, she looked at her reflection in the mirror. Locks of hair had already fallen out of her ponytail, so she pulled it out and fixed her hair again. She shoved her hands on her hips and let out a sigh. A slow smile formed across her lips as she nodded at her reflection. "Chloe Andrews is back."

She scooped her bag off the floor and headed onto the field with her teammates. Inhaling the sweet aroma of fresh-cut grass mixed with popcorn, Chloe felt the adrenaline pulsing through her veins. She skimmed the bleachers as fans filtered inside the stadium. Blinking, she noted a large group holding red signs with the number thirteen painted in black. *That's my number.*

Looking closer, she saw her mother waving her hand at Chloe. Her heart beat faster. Her family had come to cheer her on for her first game back. She lifted her hand and waved to the troop of them. It seemed half of the right side of the bleachers stood and whistled and cheered when she did.

"You have quite a fan base." Molly snickered and nudged her shoulder.

"An advantage of being one of eight."

"I'd say so."

Coach Collins motioned the girls around him. "We won

the toss. We get the ball first." They huddled around him as he went over the starting lineup and the plays he wanted to execute. Once finished, the team circled around, each member placing her hand in the center, and yelled, "Go, Cardinals!" The starters took the field.

Chloe sat on the bench. *It's okay. Wouldn't have expected to start. It's my first game back, and Molly has done well in my place.* She rubbed her hands together then blew into them. The temperature had dropped dramatically as evening approached.

She scanned the sidelines for Trevor. *I wonder where he is.* She squinted at the bleachers where her family sat, thinking he may have gone over to tell them hello. He wasn't there, either. *He'll come. He's probably here somewhere.* She unscrewed her water bottle and took a quick drink.

The game started, and Molly took control of the ball. Chloe cheered as her new friend made her way toward the opposing team's fullbacks. One of Xavier's players swiped the ball from Molly and dribbled it up the field. She kicked it to one of her team's forwards. The girl dribbled past Ball State's fullbacks and toward the goal. *Come on, Renee. You can do this.*

The player smashed the ball hard to the left. Renee's weak side. *Come on, Renee.* Chloe watched in what seemed slow motion as her roommate leaped into the air, arms extended over her head. She made impact and smacked the ball out of the goal.

"Yes!" Chloe jumped up and pumped her fist through the air. "I knew you could do it!"

The Cardinals took control of the ball again. Within no time the first half was over. Chloe patted a puffing Molly on the back. "You're having an awesome game."

Molly sucked down a drink of water. "Number forty-four's kicking my back."

"She likes to steal from the right. Keep her on the other side of you."

Molly nodded then rested her head between her knees. " 'Kay."

Chloe listened as Coach went over strategies for the second half. With the game tied, zero to zero, and Molly obviously exhausted, Chloe felt sure Coach would put her in the game. But as the clock wound down, Molly hit the field, and Chloe hit the bench.

Again.

Frustration welled inside her, and she skimmed the crowd and sidelines for Trevor. He still hadn't shown up. She couldn't imagine his missing this game. Looking toward her family, she smiled and waved. Once again they broke out into cheers for number thirteen.

The second half started and ended, and Chloe spent the duration on the bench. Ball State won, two to one. Molly scored both goals. Chloe congratulated her friend as she made her way off the field. Though she'd wanted to have a chance to play, Chloe felt truly happy for her friend.

She sat in the locker room and half listened to Coach's final comments about the game. Trevor had never shown up. But why? When Coach finished, she gathered her things and met her family at the entrance. She hugged her mom. "I didn't know you were coming."

"Mike's tournament in Indianapolis starts tomorrow, so we figured we might as well head over to Muncie and watch our favorite Cardinal."

"All right." Chloe tousled her nephew's hair. "When's his first game?"

"Nine o'clock in the morning." Sabrina hugged her sister. "We're so glad to see you."

Chloe looked at her family. "Aren't we missing a few people?"

Amanda waved her hand in the air. "Do you mean husbands and small children?"

Chloe nodded.

Gideon crossed his arms in front of his chest. "These sisters of yours decided to leave their little ones with their husbands. Their husbands decided Cameron and I had to keep an eye on the women."

Chloe burst out laughing. "So, Mike, you're the only grandchild here?"

"Yeah, but I'm hanging out with my buddies as soon as we get to the hotel," her nephew told her.

Natalie hooked her arm with Chloe's. "We thought we'd kidnap you and take you to the hotel with us."

Amanda took her bag from her hand as Kylie hooked her other arm and said, "Yep. Then we'll stay up late into the night playing board games."

Mike pointed to his chest and said again, "I'm staying in a buddy's room."

Chloe looked around at her four sisters—Kylie, Amanda, Natalie, and Sabrina—and her mom. This probably would be the only time they'd ever be able to hang out with no little ones running around. Not that she didn't love her nieces and nephews, but they did require a lot of attention.

"What about the guys?" Chloe cocked her head toward her brothers, Cameron and Gideon. "And where's Dalton?"

"Dalton had to work," said her mother.

"Really—we're not babysitting you guys." Gideon grinned. "Cameron and I are going to Danville to check out an apple orchard I'm thinking of purchasing."

"Really? That's a huge endeavor." Chloe gaped at her brother.

"That's why I'm *checking* into it. No commitments. Yet."

Chloe wrapped her arms around her mama. "I think this kidnapping sounds like a lot of fun."

&

Trevor twisted his fork through his chicken-flavored soup noodles. Long strands clung to the fork and each other until the entire bowl was twirled around his utensil. He lifted the glob to his lips and bit off a piece. It was stringy. No taste.

Dropping his fork into the bowl, he propped his elbows on the table and stared at the juice that had spilled on the floor in front of his stove. He leaned his head forward and raked his hand through his hair.

No peace. He hadn't felt peace in days.

Pulling at the collar of one of his favorite Fighting Game-cocks T-shirts from high school, the garment now felt stiff, too tight. As if it were telling him something. He huffed and pushed away from the table. Standing, he pulled off the shirt. *It's not as if I haven't gained a few pounds in the last ten years. Of course the shirt is tight.*

He walked to the washing machine and threw the shirt inside. Slamming the lid, he turned and glanced at the clock. The game had ended three hours ago. He wondered how Chloe had done. Since he hadn't had any calls from Coach Collins, he assumed her ankle held up nicely for the game. *But what did she think about me not being there?*

He knew she had to be upset with him, but he couldn't go. He'd tried. Got ready and everything. But when it came time to pick up his keys and head out the door, he couldn't do it.

He threw his hands in the air. "Lord, it's my dream job. The one I've prayed for all this time. What am I supposed to do?"

Nothing.

He slapped his hand on his thigh and walked into the living area. Flopping down in his favorite chair, he picked up his Bible and skimmed the concordance for topics he could look up to guide him, to encourage him. Something. Anything.

Nothing leaped out at him. Frustrated, he flipped through the pages, randomly opening and closing the book at different places. Finally, two words caught his attention: "Good teacher. . ." He looked at the top of the page and saw he was in the Gospel of Mark, chapter 10.

He glanced down at the passage again and read aloud. " 'Good teacher,' he asked, 'what must I do to inherit eternal life?' " Trevor continued with the words in red, the ones spoken by Christ. " 'Why do you call me good?' Jesus answered. 'No one is good—except God. You know the commandments: Do not murder. . .' "

Trevor skimmed the rest of Jesus' words as the man's next question stood out to him. " 'Teacher,' he declared, 'all these I have kept since I was a boy.' "

Trevor pushed his fingers against the words of the next verse. "Jesus looked at him and loved him." Trevor scratched his chin. Of course Jesus loved the man. He was incapable of anything less. He read on to what Jesus said. " 'One thing you lack,' he said. 'Go, sell everything you have and give to the poor, and you will have treasure in heaven. Then come, follow me.' At this the man's face fell. He went away sad, because he had great wealth."

Trevor shut his Bible and looked at the ceiling. "Lord, what does that have to do with me? I'm not a man of great wealth. I just want to know what to do about my job offer and the woman I've fallen in love with."

The phone rang. Trevor picked it up and read the caller ID. *Chloe*. He closed his eyes and held his finger away from the TALK button. What could he say to her? She'd want to know why he wasn't at the game, and he still didn't have a real answer. The answering machine picked up then beeped. Chloe's voice spilled through it. "Hey, Trevor. I don't know what happened to you tonight. I. . ." Her voice faded for a moment. "I didn't play, but Molly had a great game. We won two to one. She scored both goals. Listen. I'm going to Indianapolis with my mom and sisters." A giggle sounded. "They're kidnapping me and taking me to my nephew's soccer tournament. You can call my cell—" The answering machine clicked off, and Trevor laid the cordless phone back in its receiver.

She hadn't played, and he hadn't been there to encourage her. He was a louse. He glanced at the Fighting Gamecocks mug sitting on his coffee table. A louse still torn between the woman he loved and the job he'd always wanted.

seventeen

His mind was made up. He'd spent the last two weeks fighting with himself about what decision would be the right one. He'd finally made up his mind. Two games had passed since he'd given Chloe's ankle the necessary approval to play, but Coach had yet to put her in. He'd stood by her and encouraged her after he missed the first game she could play in, but he'd kept his distance, too. Chloe had asked him multiple times what was wrong, but he'd put her off. He had to, until he knew what he was going to do.

And now he did.

He knocked on Chloe's apartment door, hoping she was home. She answered in a sweat suit with her hair knotted on top of her head. "Trevor!" Her eyebrows lifted in surprise, and she pushed hair that had fallen from her ponytail behind her ear. "What are you doing here?"

"Two days before the last game, and I want to take you to lunch."

"Now?"

"Yep."

She bit her lip. "Can I change real quick first?"

"If you want."

She opened the door, and Trevor sat on the couch. "Where're Liz and Renee?"

"Liz is taking a nap." She placed her finger over her lips then whispered, "Renee—I don't know. Be right back."

Chloe walked down the hall, and Trevor heard a door shut.

Within moments she returned with her hair brushed straight and wearing jeans and a deep purple sweater. "You look cute."

She smiled and kissed his cheek. "Thanks."

"I thought I'd take you to Ivanhoe's." They walked to his car. Trevor opened her door then moved to his side, slipped in, and started the car.

"I've never heard of Ivanhoe's."

"You've lived in Muncie for almost four years and have never been to Ivanhoe's?"

She shrugged. "Never even heard of it."

"It's a little restaurant on the outskirts of town. It'll take us about twenty minutes to get there." He tapped the steering wheel and thought a minute. "It may not even be in Muncie, but anyway, they have the best lunch menu—and homemade ice cream, too."

"Sounds good."

"You should try the chicken salad over fruit. They add grapes and nuts to the chicken salad, giving it a great taste. And the fruit is delicious. I haven't yet tasted a sour or unripe piece."

"I'm glad I haven't eaten yet."

"For dessert I'm buying you a clown ice cream."

"A clown ice cream? What—?"

"They put a scoop of ice cream in a cup then cut a cone down the center, laying one half at the top of the ice cream like a hat. Then they put whipped cream, candies, and whatever goodies you choose on the scoop to make the clown's face. Your nephews and nieces would love it."

"Sounds fun."

He peeked at her, and she smiled. He was talking her head off. What had gotten into him? Nervousness. That's what it was. He was anxious about telling her his decision.

After pulling into the parking lot, he shut off the car, and they got out. She grabbed his hand. Her skin was soft and warm beneath his fingers. She peered up at him, and her lashes brushed her cheek when she blinked. "I'm glad you brought me."

They stood behind several couples in line. Finally, their turn came. They placed their orders, and Trevor paid for their lunch. He carried their drinks and their ticket to a booth along the wall closest to the street. She laid her purse beside her. "I can't wait to try the chicken salad."

Suddenly Trevor couldn't find words to speak. Being at Ivanhoe's made him realize the time to tell her was upon him. The cashier called their number, and Trevor picked up their tray of food and took it back to their table. He slid into his seat, and Chloe stretched her hands across to him. "Will you say grace?"

"Sure." He took her hands, his thumbs of their own volition caressing them. His prayer came out jumbled. By the time he'd said "amen," he wasn't sure if he'd even asked a blessing on their food. He wiped the back of his hand across his forehead. Tiny beads of sweat had formed. *Get a grip, Montgomery.*

Taking a deep breath, he gazed into Chloe's eyes. He opened his mouth to speak, but nothing would come. Instead, he stabbed his chicken salad with his fork and took an oversized bite. Beginning to choke, he grabbed his napkin and coughed into it.

"Are you okay?" Chloe tried to stand and leaned over the table to pat his back.

He lifted his hand and coughed once more. "I'm okay." Wiping the napkin across his mouth, he added, "I'm fine."

Chloe ate a piece of cantaloupe. "This is good."

Trevor could only respond with a nod of his head. He felt

a trickle of perspiration slip down his forehead. Brushing it away with his napkin, he exhaled through his nose. He had to get a handle on himself. He was falling apart. *This is ridiculous. You've made the decision. Just tell her.*

He opened his mouth again then looked up at her. The sweet expression on her face made his stomach flip. She laid down her fork and covered his hand with hers. "I can tell you want to say something."

"Yes, Chloe. . ." But the words wouldn't come. He frowned and swallowed the knot in his throat.

"You can tell me anything."

He tried again, but no sound left his lips.

"I'll go first." Chloe touched his cheek with her fingertip. "Trevor, I love you. I've never felt this way about anyone before." She covered her mouth with her hand then laughed. "I've said it. Trevor Montgomery, I am over-the-top in love with you."

❧

His expression fell, and Chloe realized Trevor's thoughts did not mirror hers. He shook his head. "That wasn't what I was going to say."

"Oh." She pulled her hand away from her face. Resting it on the table, she drummed her fingers on the cool, laminate-covered wood. She peered out the window and watched a lone car pass by. A knife wedged in her heart would have hurt less than his words.

She knew he had been distant the last few weeks, but she'd chalked it up to his being busy with work or whatnot. *What a fool I am.* She closed her eyes. *Why, oh why, did I blurt that out?*

Trevor's voice interrupted her thoughts. "I care about you, Chloe." His hand touched hers, and she recoiled from him.

Opening her eyes, she watched as he flattened his napkin

against the table then picked up one edge and rolled it between his fingers. His gaze seemed trained on his menial task, and he opened his mouth again to speak then clamped it shut.

She would not interrupt him this time. She'd sit still, straight, and silent, waiting for him to tell her whatever big news he had to share. Maybe that he'd found someone else. The thought crushed her, but she purposely kept her chin up.

"I've taken a job in South Carolina." He glanced up at her. "It's one I've always wanted. I'll have the same position, but it's a good increase in pay, in my hometown, close to my dad."

She folded her hands in her lap. She couldn't fault him for that. Maybe she could go with him after she graduated. The wonderful time she'd had with her mom and sisters in the hotel flooded her mind. She'd finally bonded with them. *But, Lord, I'd go if You wanted me to.*

A stirring filled her spirit. No. She was to stay. Finish school. Spend as much time with her family as she could. Besides, he wasn't asking her to go. She could hear it in his voice, see it in his eyes. He was saying good-bye. Unbidden tears pooled in her eyes. She swiped them away. "I understand."

He rubbed his forehead with his fingers. His eyes held a sadness.

She lifted her fork and scooped up a bite of chicken salad. "I really do." Putting it in her mouth, she fought back a gag. Her appetite was gone. "But I think I'd like to go home."

Trevor nodded. "Okay."

The ride home was silent. And so long. Emotion, painful and raw, constricted her lungs and scraped at her throat. Finally at her apartment, she waved good-bye and walked to her door. Unlocking it, she stepped inside, thankful no one was home.

She slipped out of her clothes and into the softest pair of

pajamas she could find. Dropping onto her bed, she picked up her remote control and turned on the television. Every station she flipped to had a couple kissing or fighting or walking or talking. She turned it off, grabbed one of her pillows, and cradled it to her.

Tears filled her eyes, and sadness filled her heart. She loved him. She really did. She'd told him, and he'd rejected her. Allowing the bitter flow of emotion, she fell face-first onto her covers. "Lord, why? Why, Lord Jesus? Why?"

She cried and called out to God until her whole body was spent. As she lay faceup on her bed, her eyelids drooped with exhaustion. Her chin quivered, and she pleaded once more. "Why, God?"

"In this world you will have trouble." The preacher's voice as he read Jesus' words that first Sunday morning she'd attended church floated through her mind. *"But take heart. I have overcome the world."*

"Dear Jesus," she whispered as she drifted off to sleep, "overcome the hurt in my heart."

eighteen

Trevor looked at his watch: 2:00 a.m. He pulled off the road and into the gas station lot. He filled up his tank then walked inside and bought an extra large cup of coffee. After dousing the liquid with several hazelnut creamers and packs of sugar, he stirred the coffee from a dark brown to a pale mud color. He lifted the cup to his lips and blew on the top. After taking a sip, he frowned then shrugged. The hot, syrupy drink would keep him awake, even if it did taste like flavored sugar.

Trudging back to his car, he wiped his eyes with the back of his hand. He'd tried to stay busy after dropping Chloe at her apartment. Went to the grocery. Washed some laundry. Flipped through television stations. Her admission of love for him assaulted him at every turn. Finally, though early in the evening, he tried to go to bed. Closing his eyes proved impossible.

After an hour of tossing and turning in his bed, Trevor had jumped up and packed his clothes. Convinced that seeing the school and his dad would cure his ailing heart and mind, he'd decided to head to South Carolina.

Noting the green road sign approaching, he tallied the hours in his mind. *I should be at Dad's by around seven o'clock. I'll slip into bed for a quick hour of shut-eye then head to church with him.* He blew on the top of his coffee then took a slow drink. *Yep, after spending a day with Dad then touring the university on Monday, I'll know my decision was the right one.*

✌

Tucking the new Bible her mother had bought her under her arm, Chloe walked into the singles' Sunday school classroom. She spied Molly and Matt sitting beside each other in the front row. They appeared deep in discussion over something Molly was pointing out in her Bible. She'd seen them discussing spiritual issues a lot lately. She hoped Matt was coming to realize his need of Jesus, and she wondered if anything more was developing, as well.

Molly looked up and motioned for Chloe to join them. She sat down beside her friend. "Hey, you two. What are we discussing today?"

"Why Jesus calls Himself a vine," Matt mumbled.

"What?"

Molly pointed to the scripture. "John 15."

"And why God says He's a gardener," added Matt.

God as a gardener was no stretch of the imagination in Chloe's opinion. Her trip with Trevor to Summit Lake had reminded her what a wonderful artist of nature He was. *Trevor.* Pain filled her heart as she opened her Bible to John 15. All night she'd contemplated telling Trevor she'd go with him to South Carolina. She felt that maybe he hadn't offered because he didn't want to put her in a position of moving farther from her family. After all, she was convinced her love for him had blossomed through God's leading, but she still couldn't find peace in telling him she'd leave. Did the feeling come from God or her own selfishness?

"Pretty much what Jesus is saying"—Molly's explanation captured Chloe's attention—"is that those who believe in Him must remain in Him, in the vine. See in verse 5 where He calls us the branches? If we, the branches, stay grafted in Him, the vine, if we stay in His Word, stay in fellowship with Him, we can do the good things He wants us to do."

Chloe shook her head gently. Following Trevor wasn't an option. She knew it to the core of her spirit. Maybe this would be a pruning time for her. She closed her eyes, thinking of her father's death, her ankle injury. Pruning was hard. It hurt.

Still, each time her mother pruned her rosebushes, the branches always grew back bigger, stronger, and with more beautiful blossoms. She had to trust God to do the same with her life.

٭

Trevor had awakened and prepared for his visit early Monday morning. The day before spent with his father had been a good one, despite the fact that his dad kept asking him what was wrong. Trevor had brushed him off with each question. Even more disconcerting was the distance he felt from God. Reading his Bible didn't help. Prayer didn't help. Even the sermon from his hometown preacher left him feeling empty.

Shaking his head, he made his way down the university walkway leading to the athletics office. Small trees dotted the campus. Some still held several fiery leaves, but much of the foliage had found its new home on the ground, dead, beneath its one-time source of life.

The lack of fullness on the branches brought an un-explained sorrow to his spirit. His heart slowed, and his legs grew heavy moving his weight across the path. A slight drizzle began to dampen his head and shoulders. Lifting his briefcase over his head, Trevor walked the last bit to the office.

He stepped inside the building and shook the water from his briefcase. Brushing the droplets from his shoulders and arms, he combed his fingers through his hair. He grabbed a mint from his pocket and slipped it in his mouth.

Finding the correct office, he stepped through the door and greeted the secretary. "Hello. I'd like to see Mr. Walter Spence."

"Do you have an appointment, Mr.—?"

"Trevor. Trevor Montgomery. I'm the new assistant athletic trainer." When the words slipped from his mouth, his stomach churned and cramped worse than any indigestion he'd ever felt.

The young woman smiled. "Mr. Spence will be thrilled. He just got to the office. Let me tell him you're here."

She disappeared into the next office. Within moments Walter Spence bounded out in front of her. "Trevor." He grabbed Trevor's hand and shook it. "What a wonderful surprise. Did you come to check out your office? Some of the people you'll be working with?"

"Actually, I've come to tell you I can't take the position."

"What?"

What? What did I just say? The knots in his stomach seemed to untie, and the heaviness in his chest began to lift. Peace flooded his heart, and he knew he'd said the right thing. A smile tugged at his lips. He covered his mouth and coughed it away. "It seems, Mr. Spence, that I'm going to have to stay at Ball State a little longer."

"Did they offer you more money?"

"No." Trevor shook his head. "Nothing like that. It's just the right place for me to be at this time." And it was. He knew it from the top of his head to the tips of his toes.

Mr. Spence crossed his arms. "This may not be the wisest of choices."

In the world's eyes, probably not. After all, he'd make more money at South Carolina, and working for his alma mater had been his goal; but it wasn't the world he was trying to impress. He wanted to stay in the will of his Lord. "Maybe not, but it's the one I have to make."

Mr. Spence's eyebrows met in a straight line. "Okay, then. I wish you the best of luck." He shook Trevor's hand again then turned and walked back into his office.

Trevor nodded to the young secretary whose mouth hung open. "Have a great day, ma'am."

He practically floated out of the office and back to his father's house. Bursting through the front door, he yelled, "Dad!" He hurried through the living room and into the kitchen. "Dad!"

"What is it?" His father stepped out of the pantry, a frown shadowing his face.

Trevor grinned. "I'm not taking the job."

"What?"

"I'm not moving to South Carolina. I'm staying at Ball State."

"Is that a good thing?"

"It's a wonderful thing." Trevor patted his dad's back. "I have so much I want to tell you. Are you able to go back to Muncie with me? Just for a few days. I'll fly you back."

His dad leaned against the cabinet and scratched his jaw. "You show up on my doorstep yesterday just before church. Now you want me to drive to Indiana with you?"

Trevor lifted his eyebrows and nodded. "Yep."

"This must be something pretty important."

Trevor laughed. "It is."

"Then what are we waiting for? I gotta pack." His father walked out of the kitchen and toward his room.

Trevor glanced at his watch. "Hurry, Dad. If we get out of here quickly, we might just make it to the second half of the game."

"Does this have anything to do with that woman you keep telling me about? The one who hurt her foot?"

"It was her ankle." Trevor rubbed his hands together with excitement. "And yes. She definitely has something to do with it."

nineteen

The last game of the season. The last game of her college career. Chloe stepped onto the field. She gazed across the long stretch of deep green grass. She looked at the goals, the white painted lines mapping penalties and boundaries. Taking in the concession stand, the bleachers, the spectators, the referees, she wanted to relish every facet of her surroundings. Relish and remember. She closed her eyes, painting the picture in her mind.

"Hustle out there!" Coach's command tore her from her memory making. She opened her eyes and rushed to the field to begin warming up with the team. Looking down at her jersey, her eyes misted. She'd been lucky thirteen since she was five years old, playing in her hometown recreational league. This was probably the last time she'd wear the number.

Not only was it the last game, but it was also senior night. She scanned the stadium for any sign of her mama. *Still not here.* A wave of sadness washed over her. Mama and Gideon would be recognized with her at halftime, but not Daddy. *I know he's dancing on streets of gold with You, though, Lord. That makes me feel better.*

Dribbling the ball, she peeked at the sidelines. Trevor wasn't there. He hadn't been at church, either. *He's probably moving to South Carolina.* She'd thought he felt something for her. After all, he even asked if she'd be his girlfriend, but it hadn't been enough.

"Chin up." Molly nudged her as she dribbled beside her.

Chloe tried to smile, but the muscles around her mouth didn't want to cooperate.

"This is your night." Molly wrapped her arm around her shoulder and squeezed.

Chloe snorted. "Yeah, but I probably won't play." She looked at Molly. "Not that I don't want you to play. I mean. . ."

"I know exactly what you mean. I bet Coach will put you in tonight."

"Don't bet on it."

"I'll ask him to."

"Don't you dare." Chloe grabbed her friend's arm. "I want to go in because Coach feels I'm needed for the team, not because you or I asked."

"We can ask God."

Chloe stared at Molly. For Chloe to go in, it almost certainly meant Molly would hit the bench, and yet her friend was willing to sacrifice, even pray that Coach would allow Chloe some time on the field.

"Hustle in, ladies!" Coach hollered from the sidelines.

"Come on." Molly extended her hands to Chloe.

Chloe hugged her friend then took hold of her hands.

"Lord," Molly began, "it's Chloe's last night of college ball. I know You have a wonderful plan for her, and You may even bless her to work with her favorite sport for years and years to come." She squeezed Chloe's hands. "It's been a rough season with her ankle injury. I remember all too well how hard it is to sit out. Tonight, precious Jesus, we ask You to allow Chloe some time in the game. Have Coach put her in then bless her on the field. We know You've heard our prayer, and we trust You with the answer, be it yes or no. We love You, Lord. Amen."

Tears slipped from Chloe's eyes as she opened them. She

noticed that tears pooled in Molly's eyes, as well. "Molly, I'm so thankful God put you in my life."

Molly hugged her. "Me, too."

Chloe scanned the field, noting the entire team had taken the bench. Coach Collins stood with his hands on his hips watching them. He popped his gum, and Chloe couldn't decipher what he thought of their quick prayer. *Maybe it will be a little nugget to lead him to You one day.*

He motioned them to the side. They hurried over and listened as he reviewed their starting play. Every senior was starting, except Chloe. Her heart sank. Molly must have felt it, because she elbowed Chloe and whispered, "We have a whole game ahead of us."

Chloe nodded and took her well-worn seat on the bench. She peered into the stands and saw an entourage of fans dressed in red and black, waving flags painted with the number thirteen. This time it appeared her entire family had made it. She smiled and waved at them. They whooped back at her. If she didn't play a single moment today, the knowledge that her whole family had come to support her filled her to the depths of her being. For the first time her family meant more than her sport, and she had never before felt so content.

If only Trevor were here. She inhaled then blew out a long breath. *I love him, Lord, but I'm going to trust him to You.*

❧

"It must be almost halftime." Trevor ran a comb through his hair then tried to press out some of the wrinkles in his pants.

"I think I hear the announcer." Vince Montgomery zipped up his jacket.

"Oh no!" Trevor started for the entrance and turned to his father. "Hurry, Dad. I want to see her be recognized." They made it to the bleachers as one of the seniors was being called. Trevor skimmed the row still waiting.

"Is she out there?"

Trevor nodded and pointed toward her. "She'll be called after one more girl. She's number thirteen." He looked up at the scoreboard's clock. "I wanted to talk to her before the second half."

"Well, get on over there."

"Let me introduce you to her family first." His words came out a bit snappier than he'd intended. His nerves were getting the best of him.

"Son." His dad touched his arm then pointed to the stands. "Her family will be easy enough to find."

"Let's go." Trevor started toward them.

His dad grabbed his arm. "No. I'll go meet the family on my own."

"But—"

"No buts. I'm fifty-one years old. I know how to make friends." He winked. "Go to your girl."

"Thanks, Dad." Trevor raced around the field to the bench where the Cardinals' team sat. He watched as Chloe's name was called and she and her mom and brother walked to the center of the field.

"She looks beautiful, huh?" Molly said beside him.

"Yeah." Trevor stared down at her. "I'm sure she's told you what I said. I was a fool. Wasn't listening to—"

Molly nodded toward the field. "Save it for her. She's coming."

Trevor looked onto the field. He and Chloe made eye contact as she walked alone toward the team. Her mom and brother had already returned to the stands. A moment of happiness flicked through her eyes, followed by hesitation and uncertainty.

"Just remember flowers and chocolate can go a long way to

win a lady's heart," Molly whispered to him. "I mean, a woman could enjoy them practically every single day of her life."

Trevor chuckled. "I'll remember that."

"Hello, Trevor." Chloe's voice was guarded. "Have you already begun your move?" She bent down, grabbed her water bottle, and took a quick drink.

"I need to talk to you." He reached for her hand. "Will you come with me for just a moment?"

She avoided his gaze. "I don't know. Coach needs—"

"It'll just take a second."

"Fine." She tossed her water bottle toward the edge of the bench.

He guided her a few yards away from the team. His mind searched for the words to say. Ten hours of driving and he hadn't figured out what to say first. He'd hurt her, and somehow he had to tell her, had to show her... *Guide me, Lord.*

"Trevor, I really have to get with my team." She started to turn away.

"Wait." She faced him, and he tried to swallow the knot in his throat. Confusion filled her expression, and he prayed his eyes showed the love he felt for her. "Chloe, I'm not moving."

She furrowed her brows. "What? Why?"

He peered out at the horizon, gazing at the deep red and pink of the beginning sunset. "I'm not supposed to move to South Carolina. I've always dreamed of the job. Always wanted to work there. When the offer came, I just figured God had given it to me. But—"

"I don't understand. You'll be closer to your dad—"

"I don't think it's what God wants. I didn't feel right about it." He took her hands and caressed their softness with his thumbs. "Don't you see? God brought you into my life."

Tears filled her eyes. One slipped down her cheek. Trevor

brushed it away with the back of his hand. Her chin quivered as she looked at the ground and whispered, "I would have prayed about going with you."

"I know, sweetheart." He cupped her chin, lifting her face to allow her gaze to meet his. "But I knew God wanted you to stay here. Finish school. See your family."

"You're right. I asked Him."

Trevor rubbed his thumb against her cheek. "I love you, Chloe Andrews. I'm not leaving you."

She smiled. "I love you, too, Trevor Montgomery."

"I still want you to be my girlfriend."

"On one condition." Chloe lifted her finger in the air.

"What's that?"

"You're not allowed to dump me again."

He glanced at her coach, who seemed to be waiting not too patiently for her return. "Never."

❧

"Molly, head out to center forward." Chloe's heart fell at Coach's words. "Chloe," he continued, "I want you at right forward."

"What?" She leaned forward, unsure she'd heard him correctly.

"Are you not able to play right forward?" he said with a growl. The tie game obviously had him feeling anxious.

"No. I'll play." Excitement coursed through her, and she looked up at Molly, who was quietly clapping her hands. Biting her lip, she jumped up and high-fived her friend.

"Let's go."

Chloe followed Molly onto the field. Peeking at the stands, she gave a short wave to her family. Trevor sat beside her mother and a man she'd never seen before. Her family's hollering drowned out the rest of the crowd.

Within moments the referee blew the whistle, and the game began again. The other team quickly dribbled the ball past Chloe. She turned and watched in trepidation as their forward made her way past Liz, as well. The girl shot hard at the goal. Relief filled Chloe when Renee caught it and kicked it back to the right side of the field.

Chloe used her chest to roll the ball to the ground so she could get control. The same girl swiped it away from Chloe and dribbled again toward Liz. Glancing to the sideline, she saw Coach pointing at her and then at his temple. He wanted her to get her head in the game.

Help me, Lord. Chloe watched as Liz stole the ball and kicked it up the center. Molly got control of the ball and dribbled a couple of steps toward the goal.

"Man on!" Chloe yelled as an opposing player ran toward Molly.

In a quick motion Molly smashed the ball with her right foot. It sailed through the air and slammed into the left side of the net. One to zero. Chloe ran over to her friend and gave her a high five before they ran back to the centerline for the opposing team to kick off.

Minutes passed as both teams fought for a goal but to no avail. Molly took control of the ball again. She dribbled toward the middle. "Man on!" Chloe yelled as the same player tried to steal the ball from Molly.

"Your turn!" Molly screamed as she kicked the ball hard to the right toward Chloe. The field was wide open except for one fullback charging from the left toward her. Chloe dribbled toward the goal. The goalie leaned left then right, preparing for Chloe's shot. Inching her way closer, Chloe twisted her hip and with all the strength she could muster kicked with her right foot.

The ball seemed to move in slow motion toward its hoped-for destination. The goalie dove toward it, and Chloe watched as she nipped it with the tip of her fingers. But the kick had been too strong, and it sailed into the net.

Score!

Chloe pumped her fist through the air as cheers erupted from the fans. Molly raced to her and wrapped her in a hug. *Thank You, God, for allowing me one more goal. Daddy, that was for you.*

Minutes later the game ended. The Cardinals had won two to zero. Chloe lined up with her team to shake hands with the opposing players. Reaching the last player, Chloe looked at the goal where she'd made the last score of her college career.

She'd spent her life striving for that goal. Her whole existence had been wrapped up in making as many soccer goals as she could tally, and she had many to her name. Looking up at the night sky, she noted that the moon's face seemed to smile down at her. The smattering of stars that brightened the sky sent her into awestruck wonder. God had given so much beauty to His creations.

She felt afresh that she was one of His precious creations. He'd formed her with a goal. One that had included a soccer field—but, more important, one that included a relationship with her Lord and Savior, Jesus. He was her ultimate goal. Her ultimate score.

twenty

May

The whistle blew, signaling the end of the recreational game. Chloe congratulated her team of young girls for their win. She waved to the opposing team's coach and her friend Liz. "Good game!" she hollered and pointed to her watch. "But I gotta hurry."

"Get going." Liz waved her away before the two teams were able to shake hands.

"Thanks." Chloe grabbed her bag and ran to her mother's car. Her mom was to rush her to the apartment to get ready for the wedding then drive Chloe back to the field in only two hours' time.

"You took long enough." Her mother cupped her cheeks and kissed her forehead. "Five minutes to and from the apartment gives us about an hour and a half to bring you back here. You don't want to be late to your own wedding."

"You're right about that. Where is everyone?"

"Some of the girls are at the apartment, though I'd say they're just about ready to head over here. The others are already at the pavilion." Mama laughed when Chloe looked back at the field. "They'll make sure everything is perfect. Now buckle your seat belt so I can get you ready."

Chloe obeyed. Within no time Chloe had showered and was sitting in a chair while her mom curled, twisted, and sprayed her hair. Her sisters had all left, and Chloe soaked in the light chatter of her mother as she worked. Growing up, Chloe rarely had time alone with her mom. She wanted to relish every moment.

"This veil is beautiful." Her mother placed it on Chloe's head. The material felt soft on her shoulders as her mom bobby-pinned it into her hair. Chloe's heart fluttered, as she knew the time drew nearer. She longed to see her soon-to-be husband, to become Mrs. Trevor Montgomery.

Her mother opened the makeup kit and started applying blush to Chloe's cheeks. Many women spent their wedding day getting ready in some beauty parlor. Chloe had spent hers coaching a soccer game. It didn't matter to Chloe. No one fixed her up as well as her mama. Dotting her lips with gloss, Mama stood away from her. "Gorgeous. Now stand up and let's get you into that dress."

Chloe stepped into her dress and lifted it up over her. She turned, and her mother zipped up the dress then buttoned the multiple pearls that covered the zipper. Gently bending down, she slipped on her low-heeled shoes.

She stood to her full height and faced her mother. "Well?"

Mama covered her mouth with her hands. Tears glistened in her eyes, and she shook her head. "You're so beautiful." She embraced Chloe. "Daddy would have been so proud of you."

Closing her eyes, Chloe thought of her daddy's reaction when he'd seen each of her sisters for the first time in their wedding dresses. She envisioned him responding the same with her. "I wish Daddy could be here, too."

"We won't be sad." Mama pushed one of Chloe's curls behind her shoulder. "God has blessed you with a wonderful man, and I believe his father will treat you as if you were his own daughter." She touched Chloe's cheek. "You always needed your daddy. God's blessed you with a second one."

No one could ever replace her daddy, but Mama was right. God had blessed her with Vince, and he loved her as if she were his own child. He'd even agreed to walk her down the aisle. "I know, Mama."

Chloe looked in the mirror for the first time. She did look beautiful. Her blue eyes glowed beneath the soft browns and pinks Mama had dusted on her eyelids. The light pink lipstick was just enough to add a bit of color to her lips. Her long brown hair was swept up into a high clip with tendrils of curls rolling down her shoulders and back. "Mama, I'm going to have you fix me up every day."

"We need to go." Mama looked at her watch and grabbed Chloe's hand. "My baby's getting married in thirty minutes."

They drove back to the soccer field. Chloe walked carefully toward the pavilion, trying hard to hide from Trevor's sight until the wedding. She looked around the corner of the cinder-block restrooms and saw Trevor, her brothers, Matt, and their preacher standing on the soccer field beneath one of the goals.

Her sisters had decorated the goal with wildflowers of every color—yellow, pink, purple, white, blue, and even splashes of red. Chairs were lined up in rows on the field. An aisle had been made between them to allow her bridal march. She'd wanted a wedding that showed God's wonderful, natural creations—trees, green grass, blue sky, flowers that grew on their own in nature. She'd also wanted to wed at the place where she'd spent most of her life, the place God had used to lead her to Trevor—a soccer field.

Her sisters and Molly rushed to her. The soft red dresses looked lovely on them. She hadn't wanted to choose between her married sisters, so she'd asked them all to be matrons of honor and Molly her maid of honor.

"You look beautiful." Molly fluffed the bottom of her veil.

"I'd say." Trevor's dad walked up behind her. "It's just about time." He offered his arm. "Ready?"

"Oh yes."

૨૦

Trevor knew at any moment his heart would burst from his chest. He'd never been so excited and nervous at the same time. He watched as Sabrina, then Natalie, made her way down the aisle. Kylie followed, then Amanda. "I can't take it. There're too many of them," Trevor whispered to Matt.

"Hey, I heard that," Dalton said beside Matt. "I agree."

Trevor bit back a chuckle as Molly made her way down the aisle. He glanced at Matt. His friend's eyes glowed at the sight of his fiancé. Matt had accepted Christ a short time after the season ended. He and Molly had been an item ever since. In fact, Trevor and Chloe would be in their wedding in just a few months.

The "Wedding March" played from the sound system they'd set up behind him. Finally. It was time for his bride. His dad and Chloe stepped out from behind the pavilion.

She took his breath away. Her long, straight white dress hugged her curves to perfection. A thin diamond necklace sparkled in the sun, drawing his attention to her slender neck and collarbone. Beautiful. He longed to see her face beneath her veil. His dad needed to hurry up, needed to get his bride down that aisle and into Trevor's arms.

They stopped a few feet in front of him. The preacher's words sounded like gibberish as he waited for his father to lift her veil. He had to see her. Had to look into her eyes. Had to see the slight curve of her lips. He clasped his hands, trying to fight the urge to throw her over his shoulder and declare her his own.

His dad touched the veil. Slowly, so achingly slowly, he lifted the tulle away from her face. Trevor took her hand in his, gazing into her eyes. The storm simmering in them was one of passion and promise, electrifying and stirring. "Wow! You're beautiful," he whispered before they faced the preacher.

Within moments they recited their vows of love, today and forever, no matter the circumstances. Trevor focused on his words of promise. He drank in the sincere inflection in her voice, the way her gaze never parted from his, the slow nodding of her head as she recited her vows. For as long as he lived, he would stay committed to her.

At one time he had believed his dream was in South Carolina. God showed him a new dream, a better one, one that would fill his days with happiness and his nights with warmth. One that came from the Lord Himself.

"I now pronounce you man and wife," the preacher's voice boomed into the air. "You may kiss your bride."

Trevor lowered his lips to hers. Their sweetness beckoned him to kiss her a second time. *Thank You, Lord, that the dreams You give are so much better than the ones I think up.*

❧

Chloe stood beside the table of finger foods under the pavilion. She picked up a piece of cheese and slipped it into her mouth. Having not eaten since well before lunch, she was famished. She gazed at her new husband, standing with her brothers.

He smiled at her, and her heart beat faster. She watched as he excused himself from them and made his way to her. "You look happy, Mrs. Montgomery." He lifted her chin and gently kissed her lips.

She closed her eyes. "I think I could hear that said every day for the rest of my life."

"You will." His longing to be alone was evident in his voice.

She reached up and touched his cheek. "This has been the most perfect wedding."

He chuckled. "That's because it included you." He bent down and kissed the tip of her nose.

"And you." She tilted her head up and kissed his lips. Looking past him, she saw the soccer goal covered in flowers of various shades. She'd sought after that goal all her life. Worked for it. Sweated for it. Yearned for it.

She'd given her life to God. He was in control now. In His amazing grace, when she wasn't even looking, He'd given her a man who exceeded her dreams. God had even given her the position of coaching the girls' soccer team at Muncie Central High School in the fall.

"You're thinking awfully hard." Trevor reached for her hand and kissed her knuckles. "What thoughts are running through that beautiful mind of yours?"

"That I'm finally pursuing the right goal."

"Oh?" Trevor's eyebrows furrowed into a straight line, and he looked at the goal where they'd wed.

"I'm after God's goals for my life." She turned his face until their gazes met. Reaching up to him, she caressed his cheek with her hand. "I praise Him that His goal includes you."

A Letter To Our Readers

Dear Reader:

In order that we might better contribute to your reading enjoyment, we would appreciate your taking a few minutes to respond to the following questions. We welcome your comments and read each form and letter we receive. When completed, please return to the following:

Fiction Editor
Heartsong Presents
PO Box 719
Uhrichsville, Ohio 44683

1. Did you enjoy reading *Pursuing the Goal* by Jennifer Johnson?
   ❑ Very much! I would like to see more books by this author!
   ❑ Moderately. I would have enjoyed it more if

   _____

   _____

   _____

2. Are you a member of **Heartsong Presents**? ❑ Yes ❑ No
   If no, where did you purchase this book? _____

   _____

3. How would you rate, on a scale from 1 (poor) to 5 (superior), the cover design? _____

4. On a scale from 1 (poor) to 10 (superior), please rate the following elements.

   ____ Heroine   ____ Plot
   ____ Hero   ____ Inspirational theme
   ____ Setting   ____ Secondary characters

5. These characters were special because? _____

_____

_____

6. How has this book inspired your life? _____

_____

_____

7. What settings would you like to see covered in future
   Heartsong Presents books? _____

_____

_____

8. What are some inspirational themes you would like to see
   treated in future books? _____

_____

_____

9. Would you be interested in reading other **Heartsong
   Presents** titles? ❏ Yes   ❏ No

10. Please check your age range:
   ❏ Under 18   ❏ 18-24
   ❏ 25-34   ❏ 35-45
   ❏ 46-55   ❏ Over 55

Name _____

Occupation _____

Address _____

City, State, Zip_____

Heartsong

Any 12
Heartsong
Presents titles
for only
$27.00*

CONTEMPORARY ROMANCE IS CHEAPER BY THE DOZEN!

Buy any assortment of twelve *Heartsong Presents* titles and save 25% off the already discounted price of $2.97 each!

*plus $3.00 shipping and handling per order and sales tax where applicable.
If outside the U.S. please call
740-922-7280 for shipping charges.

HEARTSONG PRESENTS TITLES AVAILABLE NOW:

___HP505 *Happily Ever After,*
            M. Panagiotopoulos
___HP506 *Cords of Love,* L. A. Coleman
___HP509 *His Christmas Angel,* G. Sattler
___HP510 *Past the Ps Please,* Y. Lehman
___HP513 *Licorice Kisses,* D. Mills
___HP514 *Roger's Return,* M. Davis
___HP517 *The Neighborly Thing to Do,*
            W. E. Brunstetter
___HP518 *For a Father's Love,* J. A. Grote
___HP521 *Be My Valentine,* J. Livingston
___HP522 *Angel's Roost,* J. Spaeth
___HP525 *Game of Pretend,* J. Odell
___HP526 *In Search of Love,* C. Lynxwiler
___HP529 *Major League Dad,* K. Y'Barbo
___HP530 *Joe's Diner,* G. Sattler
___HP533 *On a Clear Day,* Y. Lehman
___HP534 *Term of Love,* M. Pittman Crane
___HP537 *Close Enough to Perfect,* T. Fowler
___HP538 *A Storybook Finish,* L. Bliss
___HP541 *The Summer Girl,* A. Boeshaar
___HP542 *Clowning Around,* W. E. Brunstetter
___HP545 *Love Is Patient,* C. M. Hake
___HP546 *Love Is Kind,* J. Livingston
___HP549 *Patchwork and Politics,* C. Lynxwiler
___HP550 *Woodhaven Acres,* B. Etchison
___HP553 *Bay Island,* B. Loughner
___HP554 *A Donut a Day,* G. Sattler
___HP557 *If You Please,* T. Davis
___HP558 *A Fairy Tale Romance,*
            M. Panagiotopoulos
___HP561 *Ton's Vow,* K. Cornelius
___HP562 *Family Ties,* J. L. Barton
___HP565 *An Unbreakable Hope,* K. Billerbeck
___HP566 *The Baby Quilt,* J. Livingston
___HP569 *Ageless Love,* L. Bliss
___HP570 *Beguiling Masquerade,* C. G. Page
___HP573 *In a Land Far Far Away,*
            M. Panagiotopoulos

___HP574 *Lambert's Pride,* L. A. Coleman and
            R. Hauck
___HP577 *Anita's Fortune,* K. Cornelius
___HP578 *The Birthday Wish,* J. Livingston
___HP581 *Love Online,* K. Billerbeck
___HP582 *The Long Ride Home,* A. Boeshaar
___HP585 *Compassion's Charm,* D. Mills
___HP586 *A Single Rose,* P. Griffin
___HP589 *Changing Seasons,* C. Reece and
            J. Reece-Demarco
___HP590 *Secret Admirer,* G. Sattler
___HP593 *Angel Incognito,* J. Thompson
___HP594 *Out on a Limb,* G. Gaymer Martin
___HP597 *Let My Heart Go,* B. Huston
___HP598 *More Than Friends,* T. H. Murray
___HP601 *Timing is Everything,* T. V. Bateman
___HP602 *Dandelion Bride,* J. Livingston
___HP605 *Picture Imperfect,* N. J. Farrier
___HP606 *Mary's Choice,* Kay Cornelius
___HP609 *Through the Fire,* C. Lynxwiler
___HP610 *Going Home,* W. E. Brunstetter
___HP613 *Chorus of One,* J. Thompson
___HP614 *Forever in My Heart,* L. Ford
___HP617 *Run Fast, My Love,* P. Griffin
___HP618 *One Last Christmas,* J. Livingston
___HP621 *Forever Friends,* T. H. Murray
___HP622 *Time Will Tell,* L. Bliss
___HP625 *Love's Image,* D. Mayne
___HP626 *Down From the Cross,* J. Livingston
___HP629 *Look to the Heart,* T. Fowler
___HP630 *The Flat Marriage Fix,* K. Hayse
___HP633 *Longing for Home,* C. Lynxwiler
___HP634 *The Child Is Mine,* M. Colvin
___HP637 *Mother's Day,* J. Livingston
___HP638 *Real Treasure,* T. Davis
___HP641 *The Pastor's Assignment,* K. O'Brien
___HP642 *What's Cooking,* G. Sattler
___HP645 *The Hunt for Home,* G. Aiken
___HP646 *On Her Own,* W. E. Brunstetter

(If ordering from this page, please remember to include it with the order form.)

Presents

Great Inspirational Romance at a Great Price!

Heartsong Presents books are inspirational romances in contemporary and historical settings, designed to give you an enjoyable, spirit-lifting reading experience. You can choose wonderfully written titles from some of today's best authors like Wanda E. Brunstetter, Mary Connealy, Susan Page Davis, Cathy Marie Hake, Joyce Livingston, and many others.

When ordering quantities less than twelve, above titles are $2.97 each.
Not all titles may be available at time of order.